Suddenly a shadow ⬚⬚⬚⬚⬚⬚⬚⬚⬚⬚⬚⬚⬚⬚⬚⬚⬚⬚⬚⬚⬚ ⬚nced up with a terrible start a⬚ ⬚⬚⬚ ⬚⬚⬚ing glimpse of great fanged jaws and glowing eyes that glared from a hideous head; a thick red tongue licked out in unholy desire, and a spray of saliva rained down upon their transparent metal helmets and leatherlike clothes.

And then Barbara's leather-covered hands bit like sharp stones into his arm; he felt himself dragged over the edge.

They landed unhurt among the loose pile of branches below. A great mad clawing and horrible bass mewing above them whipped them to desperate speed. They made it just as that enormous head peered down from the second level of the cave, visible only by the phosphorescent glow of its eyes, like two burning coals.

There was a terrific scrambling sound behind them as they pushed wildly down to the next level; and then, abruptly, silence and continuing darkness.

"What's happened?" Jamieson asked in bewilderment.

There was bitterness in Barbara's voice as she said, "It knows we can't get out. We're finished."

THE WAR AGAINST THE RULL

by

A. E. van Vogt

ace books

A Division of Charter Communications Inc.
A GROSSET & DUNLAP COMPANY
1120 Avenue of the Americas
New York, New York 10036

I

As THE SPACESHIP vanished into the steamy mists of Eristan II, Trevor Jamieson drew his gun. He felt dizzy, sickened by the way he had been tossed and buffeted for long moments in the furious wind stream of the great ship. But awareness of danger held him tense there in the harness that was attached by cables to the antigravity plate above him. With narrowed eyes, he stared up at the ezwal which was peering down at him over the edge of the still swaying skyraft.

Its three-in-line eyes, as gray as dully polished steel, gazed at him, unwinking; its massive blue head poised alertly and—Jamieson knew—ready to jerk back the instant it read in his thoughts an intention of shooting.

"Well," said Jamieson harshly, "here we are, both of us—thousands of light-years from our respective home planets. And we're falling down into a primitive hell! that you, with only your isolated life on Carson's Planet to judge by, cannot begin to imagine despite your ability to read my thoughts. Even a six-thousand-pound ezwal can't survive down there alone."

A great claw-studded paw slid over the side of the raft, flicked down at one of the three slender cables that supported Jamieson's harness. There was a bright, steely *ping* as the cable parted from the slashing blow, and the force of it lifted Jamieson in his harness several feet. He dropped back heavily and began swinging from the two remaining cables as from a trapeze. Awkwardly, gun in hand, he craned his neck to defend these last two supports from attack.

But the ezwal made no further threatening move, and there was only the great head and the calm, unwinking eyes peering down at him. Finally, a thought penetrated to Jamieson. A thought cool and unhurried: "At the moment I have only one concern. Of the hundred or more men on your ship, only you remain alive. Out of all the human race, therefore, only you know that the ezwals of what you call Carson's Planet are not senseless beasts but intelligent beings. Your government, we know, is having great difficulty in settling or keeping colonists on our planet, because we are regarded simply as a sort of natural force, very dangerous to cope with but unavoidable. That is just the way we want the situation to remain. Once human beings became convinced that we are an intelligent enemy, there would be a systematic, full-scale warfare against us. This would handicap us seriously in our unalterable purpose of driving all trespassers from our world. Because you know this, rather than take the slightest risk of your escaping the jungle dangers below, I took the chance of jumping on top of this antigravity raft just as you were launching yourself out of the lock."

"What makes you so sure," asked Jamieson, "that finishing me off will settle the matter? Have you forgotten the other ship with two ezwals aboard, a female and her young? At last contact, it was undamaged by the Rull warship that wrecked this one, and it is probably on its way to Earth right now."

"I am aware of that," returned the ezwal contemptuously. "And I am also aware of the frank disbelief on the part of its commander when you merely hinted that ezwals might be more intelligent than most human beings suspected. You alone might be able to convince Earth's government of the truth, because you alone are certain. As for the other ezwals you have captured, they will never betray their kind."

"Ezwals may not be quite as altruistic as you indicate," said Jamieson cynically. "After all, you saved your own life when you jumped on this antigravity raft. You would not have been able to operate a lifeboat, so you would have crashed with the ship by now, and I doubt that even an ezwal could—"

His voice collapsed in an *ugh* of amazement as in a blur of motion the ezwal twisted up, a rearing, monstrous blue shape of frightful fangs and edged claws that reached at a gigantic bird. On huddled, tentlike wings, the bird was diving straight down at the raft. It did not swoop aside. Jamieson had a brief, terrifying glimpse of its protruding eyes and of the sicklelike talons, tensing for the thrust at the ezwal.

The crash as it struck the ezwal set the raft tossing like a chip in stormy waters. Jamieson swung with dizzy speed from side to side. Gusts of sound from the smashing beat of those great wings were like thunderclaps about his head. Gasping, he raised his gun. The white flame of it reached toward one of those wings and made a dark smear across it. The wing drooped, and, simultaneously, the bird was flung from the raft by the raging strength of the ezwal. It plunged down, and down, turning slowly, until it became lost against the dark background of the land mass below.

A grating sound above him made Jamieson look up quickly. The ezwal, dangerously off balance, teetered at the very edge of the raft, with its four upper limbs pawing the air uselessly. The remaining two fought with bitter effort at the metal bars on top of the raft—and won. The great body drew back, until, once again, only the massive head was visible. Jamieson lowered his gun in grim good humor.

"You see," he said, "even a bird was almost too much

for us—and I could have burned your belly open. I didn't because of the simple fact that I need you—and you need me. Here is the situation: As nearly as I can reckon, the ship will have crashed by now on the mainland not far beyond the Demon Straits, a body of water about twenty miles wide which separates this great island from that mainland. We got out of that falling ship none too soon; in another minute or so, the slip stream would have made it impossible. But now our only chance of rescue is to get to it again. It has stores of food, and it will provide shelter against some of the most insensately feral animal life in the known galaxy. I might just possibly be able to repair the sub-space radio—or even one of the lifeboats.

"But to get there will take all the resources both of us can muster. First, fifty miles or more of hostile, dense jungle between here and the Demon Straits. Then to build a navigable raft large enough to protect us from sea monsters that could swallow you whole. All your tremendous strength and fighting ability, plus your telepathic powers, all my skill, plus my atomic weapon, will be needed to get us through. What do you say?"

There was no answer. Jamieson slid his gun into its holster. It would do no good to damage with his weapon the one being that could help him escape. He could only hope that the ezwal would be equally careful not to hurt him.

A warm, wet wind breathed against his body, bringing the first faint, obscene odors from below. The raft was still at a great height, yet through the steamy mists that pervaded this primeval land patches of jungle and sea showed more clearly now—a patternless sprawl of dark trees alternating with water that glimmered in the probing sunlight.

Minute by minute the scene grew vaster and more fantastic. To the north, as far as the eye could see among the coiling vapors, spread the dank tangle of vegetation. Somewhere in the dimness beyond, Jamieson knew, lay the ugly swell of water called the Demon Straits. It all added up to the endless, deadly reality that was Eristan II.

"Since you're not answering." continued Jamieson softly, "I must guess that you think you're going to get through by yourself. All your long life, all the long generations of your ancestors, you and your kind have depended entirely on your magnificent bodies for survival. While men herded fearfully in their caves, discovering fire as a partial protection, desperately creating weapons that had never before existed, always a bare jump ahead of violent death—all those hundreds of centuries, the ezwal of Carson's Planet roamed his great, fertile continents, unafraid, matchless in strength as in intellect, needing no homes, no fires, no clothing, no weapons, no—"

"Adaptation to a difficult environment," the ezwal interrupted coolly, "is a logical goal of the superior being. Human beings have created what they call civilization, which is in fact merely a material barrier between themselves and their environment. This barrier is so complex and unwieldy that merely keeping it going occupies the entire existence of the race. Individually, man is a frivolous, unsuspecting *slave*, who spends his life in utter subservience to artificiality and dies wretchedly of some flaw in his disease-ridden body. And it is this arrogant weakling with his insatiable will to dominance that is the greatest existing danger to the sane, self-reliant races of the Universe!"

Jamieson laughed curtly. "But you will perhaps agree that even by your own standards there is something commendable about an insignificant manifestation of life which has fought successfully against all odds, aspired to all knowledge and finally attained the stars!"

9

"Nonsense!" The answer held overtones of brittle impatience. "Man and his thoughts constitute a disease. As proof, during the past few minutes, you have been offering specious arguments to lead once more to an appeal for my assistance. A characteristic example of human dishonesty.

"As further evidence," the ezwal continued, "I need but anticipate the moment of our landing. Assuming that I make no attempt to harm you, nevertheless your pitiful body will be in deadly danger continually, while I—well, you must admit that, though there may be beasts below physically stronger than I, the difference cannot be so great that my intelligence would not more than balance the situation. Actually, I question that there is to be found below a single beast both stronger and faster than I."

"A single beast, no," said Jamieson patiently. He felt tense and anxious, conscious that every argument he projected could mean life or death. "But, for example, your own well-populated planet would appear desolate by comparison with this one. Even a well-trained, well-armed soldier cannot long stand alone against a mob."

The response was immediate. "By that reasoning, neither could two. Especially if one is crippled by heredity and would present more handicap than help to the other despite the possession of a weapon that he relies upon much too heavily."

Jamieson struggled to control his exasperation. He pressed on. "I am not stressing the importance of my weapon, although it should not be underrated. The important thing—"

"Is your great intelligence, I suppose," came the retort, "which prompts you to protract a futile argument indefinitely."

"Not *my* intelligence," Jamieson said urgently. "I mean *our* intelligence. I mean the advantage of—"

"What you mean is unimportant. You have convinced me that you will not escape alive from the island below. Therefore—"

This time, two great arms flashed downward in a single coordinated gesture. The two remaining cables attached to Jamieson's harness parted like mere strings. So mighty was the blow that Jamieson was flung upward and outward in a hundred-foot arc before his taut body began to descend through the moist, heavy air.

A thought, cool with irony, struck after him: "I observe that you are a provident man, Trevor Jamieson, in having not only a knapsack but a parachute strapped to your back. This should enable you to reach the ground safely. From that point on, you will be free to exercise your argumentative powers on any jungle denizens you chance to meet. Goodbye!"

Jamieson pulled the ripcord, clenched his teeth and waited. For an awful moment there was no slackening whatever in his fall. He twisted awkwardly to look, wondering if the chute had become fouled with one of the three broken cables still attached to his harness. His first glance brought a wave of relief. It was beginning to pull sluggishly from the pack. It had been thoroughly dampened, evidently, by the extreme humidity, and even after it opened, several seconds passed before it billowed full above him.

Jamieson unsnapped the cable remnants from his harness and flung them away. He was now falling at a very moderate speed due to the dense air—nearly eighteen pounds per square inch at sea level. He grimaced. Sea level was where he would be all too quickly now.

There was, he saw, no sea immediately beneath him. A few splotches of water, yes, and a straggle of trees. The rest was a sort of clearing. except that it wasn't, exactly. It had a grayish, repellent appearance. The shock of recognition came suddenly and drained the blood from his cheeks. Quagmire! An unfathomable sea of slimy, clinging mud! In panic he tore at the lines of his parachute, as if by sheer physical strength he would draw himself toward the jungle—that jungle so near yet too far by (he made a quick calculation) a quarter of a mile. He groaned and cringed in anticipation of the foul suffocating oblivion that was now only minutes away.

The sheer deadliness of the danger galvanized him. Jamieson began to manipulate the chute carefully for maximum drift. Abruptly, he saw that the solid mass of trees was beyond his reach. The parachute was less than five hundred feet above that deadly, mottled expanse of mud. The jungle itself was about the same distance to the northwest. To reach it would require at least a forty-five-degree descent—an impossibility without wind. Even as he had the thought, he felt the faintest of breezes lift the parachute slightly and waft it closer to the goal. As suddenly as it had come, the wind died. And it had not made enough difference.

The crisis was approaching swiftly. The edge of the jungle was two hundred feet away, then a hundred, and then he saw that his feet would hit the gray-green, stagnant mud in seconds. He lifted them as high as he could, at the same time running his hands up the twin groups of lines from where they converged into the harness. With a tremendous effort, he wrapped them around his fists and raised his whole body the length of his arms. Still not enough. His knees plowed into the slime a full thirty feet from the undergrowth marking the nearest solid ground.

Instantly, he flattened himself out on the yielding surface to distribute his weight, although the strong, brackish odor of the mire close to his face made breathing difficult. Before the parachute could spill all its air, he released his short grip on the lines so that it would be carried as far as possible away from him. There was just a chance that . . .

His luck did not run out yet. The limp parachute festooned itself among the nearest group of bushes. It did not come free at his gentle tug. He But his body was already half immersed in the soft, sucking mud. He jerked tentatively a few times on the lines, then pulled firmly. The mud clung to him with deadly insistence.

Desperate, Jamieson hauled on the lines as hard as he could. His body came partly free; at the same time there was a tearing sound from the parachute, and the lines went slack. Jamieson shakily gathered them in until there was resistance, then pulled hard again. This time his body moved more easily. Two more pulls and he was sliding over the bubbling surface.

Keeping an even strain on the lines, he drew himself forward, hand over hand until at long last the tough roots of a shrub came within his grasp. In a final, frenzied burst of energy born of revulsion, he forced his way, scrambling through the branches of the shrub and flung himself against the parachute where it hung in folds over a tall bush. The bush bent double with his weight, then held him, swaying. For several minutes he lay there prone, almost unaware of his surroundings.

When he did look around, it was to receive a disappointment—one that was all the more keen because of what he had just been through. He was on a little island separated from the main bulk of forest by nearly a hundred feet of quagmire. The island was about thirty feet long by twenty wide; five trees, the tallest about thirty feet high, maintained a precarious existence on its soggy yet comparatively firm base.

The negative feeling yielded to hope. The combined height of the five trees represented a total of over a hundred feet. Definitely enough length. But— His first glow of hope faded. There was a small hatchet in his knapsack. He had a mental picture of himself felling those trees with it, trimming them and sliding them endwise into place. It would be a long and arduous task.

Jamieson sat down, conscious for the first time of a dull ache in his shoulders, the strained tenseness of his whole body and the oppressive heat. He could barely see the sun, a white blob in the misty sky, but it was almost straight overhead. That meant, on this rather slowly rotating planet, there would be about twelve hours until dark. He sighed with the realization that he had better take advantage of the relative safety of this isolated spot and rest a while. As he selected a nook screened by overhanging bushes he was extremely mindful of the gargantuan bird of prey encountered earlier. He stretched out on the damp turf and rolled under a canopy of leaves.

The heat was bearable here, though the shade was scattered. The sky glared whitely from all directions. It hurt his eyes and he closed them. He must have slept. When he opened his eyes it took a moment to locate the sun. It had moved some distance toward the horizon. Two hours at least, perhaps three. Jamieson stirred, stretched and realized that he felt refreshed. His mind stopped as he came to that realization—stopped from the shock of a staggering discovery.

A bridge of fallen trees, thicker, more solid than any on the little island stretched straight and strong across the mud to the jungle beyond. Jamieson's brain started functioning again. There could, after all, be little doubt as to who had performed that colossal feat. And yet, even though his guess had to be correct, he felt a vague, primordial panic as the blue saurianlike bulk of the ezwal reared above the bushes and three eyes of dull steel turned toward him. A thought came: "You need

14

have no fear, Trevor Jamieson. On reconsideration, your point of view seemed to contain some merit. I will assist you for the time being, and—"

Jamieson's harsh laugh cut off the thought. "What you mean is that you've run up against something you couldn't handle. Since you're pretending to be altruistic, I guess I'll have to wait to find out what happened." He shouldered his knapsack and started toward the bridge. "In the meantime, we have a long way to go."

II

THE GIANT SNAKE slid heavily out of the jungle, ten feet from the mainland end of the bridge of trees and thirty feet to the left of the ezwal, which had already crossed over. Jamieson, shuffling toward the center of the bridge, had seen the first violent swaying of the long, purple-edged grass and now froze where he was as the broad, ugly head reared into sight, followed by the first twenty feet of yellowish, glistening body, fully a yard thick. For a brief moment the great head was turned directly at him. Its little pig eyes seemed to glare straight into his own.

Shock held Jamieson—shock and utter dismay at the incredibly bad luck that had allowed this deadly creature to find him in such a helpless position. His paralysis there, under those blazing eyes, was an agonizing thing—an uncontrollable tautness that strained every muscle. But it worked. The fearsome head whipped aside, fixed in eager fascination on the ezwal, and took on a new rigidity. Jamieson relaxed somewhat; his fear became tinged with anger. He projected a scathing thought at the ezwal: "I understood that you could sense the approach of dangerous beasts by reading their minds."

No answer came to him. The monstrous snake flowed farther into the clearing, the flat, horned head gliding smoothly above the long, undulating body. The ezwal backed slowly, yielding reluctantly to the plain fact that it was no match for this vast creature.

Calmer now, Jamieson directed another thought at the ezwal: "It may interest you to know that as chief scientist for the Interstellar Military Commission, I received a report on Eristan II not too long ago. In the opinion of our survey expedition, its value as a military base is very doubtful, and there were two main reasons: one of the damnedest flesh-eating plants you ever heard of and this pretty baby. There are millions of both of them. Each snake breeds hundreds in its lifetime—their numbers are limited only by the food supply, which is potentially every other species on the planet, so they can't be stamped out. They attain a length of about a hundred and fifty feet and a weight of eight tons. Unlike most of the other killers on this planet, they hunt by day."

The ezwal, now some fifty feet away from the snake and still backing slowly, sent Jamieson a swift series of thoughts: "Its appearance did surprise me, but only because its mind held merely a vague curiosity about some sounds—no clear intention to kill. But that's unimportant; it's here; it's dangerous. It doesn't think it can get me, but it's considering the chances, in a rudimentary way. In spite of its desire for me, the problem remains essentially yours; the danger is *all* yours."

Jamieson was grim. "Don't be too sure that you're not in danger. That fellow looks muscle-bound, but when he starts moving, he's like a steel spring for the first three or four hundred feet."

An impression of arrogant self-assurance accompanied the ezwal's retort. "I can run four hundred feet before you can count your fingers."

"*Into that jungle?* Twenty feet from the edge, it's like a mat—or, rather, like one mat after another. In spite of that, I've no doubt you could drive that big body of yours through it. But nowhere near as fast as the snake, which is built for the purpose. It might possibly lose a prey as small as me, in that tangle, but in your case—"

"And why," interposed the ezwal, "should I be so foolish as to head into the jungle when I can skirt the edge of it without hindrance?"

"*Because,*" Jamieson returned, with chilling emphasis, "*you'd be running into a trap.* If I recall the lay of the land as I saw it from the air, the jungle tapers out into a narrow point not many hundreds of feet behind you. I wouldn't gamble that the snake isn't smart enough to take advantage of that fact."

There was startled silence; finally: "Why don't you turn your atomic gun on it—burn it?"

"And have it come out here while I'm burning through that tough head to that small brain? These snakes live half their lives in this mud and move around on it as well as anywhere. Sorry, I cannot take him on by myself."

The brief seconds that passed then were heavy with tension—and reluctance. But there could be no delay, as the ezwal must have known. Sure enough, the grudging request came through: "I am open to suggestions —*and hurry!*"

The depressing realization came to Jamieson that the ezwal was once more asking for his assistance *knowing* that it would be given yet was offering no promise in return. And there was no time for bargaining. Curtly he projected: "We must act as a team. Before the snake attacks, its head will start swaying. That's almost a universal reptilian method of hypnotizing victims into paralysis. Actually, the motion is partially self-hypnotizing, since it concentrates the snake's attention on its intended victim. A few seconds after it begins to sway, I'll burn it in the region of the eyes, which will damage or destroy its vision. Then you get on its back—fast! Its brain is located just behind that great horn. Claw your way there, and bite in if you can, while I try to weaken it by an attack on its body. *It's starting now!*"

The tremendous head had begun to move. Jamieson raised his gun slowly, fighting to steady his trembling hand. When he was sure of his aim, he squeezed the control button.

It was not so much, then, that the snake put up an awesome fight as that it wouldn't die. Its smoking remains were still twisting half an hour later when Jamieson stumbled weakly from the bridge of trees and slumped to the ground. When finally he climbed to his feet, the ezwal was sitting fifty feet away along the narrow strand, contemplating him. It looked strangely sleek and beautiful in its blue coat and in the supple massiveness of its form. There was comfort for him in the knowledge that, for the time being at least, the mighty muscles that rippled underneath that smooth hide were on his side.

He returned the ezwal's stare steadily. Finally he said, "What happened to the antigravity raft?"

"I abandoned it about thirty of your miles north of here."

Jamieson hesitated; then: "We'll have to go to it. I practically depowered my gun on that snake. It needs a breeder reactor for recharging, and the only one this side of the ship is the small one on that raft. We'll need it again, I'm sure you'll agree."

There was no answer. Jamieson hesitated, then spoke decisively. "The obvious method of getting there quickly is for me to ride on your back. I can get my parachute rig from the little island and contrive a sort of harness for your neck and forelegs to hold myself in place. What do you say?"

This time there was sensory evidence of mental squirming before the proud beast could acquiesce. "Undoubtedly," it projected at last, contemptuously, "that would be a method of transporting a weak body such as yours. Very well, get your harness."

A few minutes later Jamieson approached the ezwal with a boldness he didn't feel and unrolled the bundled parachute on the ground beside it. At close range the ezwal's great bulk was truly imposing—even surprising, since, at a distance. its suppleness and ease of movement tended to make it look smaller. Jamieson felt puny indeed as he set about the strange business of making a harness for this six-legged behemoth.

Again and again as he touched its body Jamieson felt a faint wave of repugnance emanating from its mind.

"That ought to do it," he said finally, surveying his handiwork. He had wrapped the light, strong lines of that parachute with the cloth for padding and crisscrossed them under the beast's body between the fore- and middle-legs, making a close-fitting harness that would allow the ezwal full freedom of movement. Attached just behind the neck, the straps of his original harness made rude but effective stirrups.

Once on the ezwal's back, Jamieson felt a little less vulnerable.

"Before we go," he said softly, "what did you run into that made you change your mind? I have an idea—"

He was almost flung from his perch by the ezwal's

first great bound, and thereafter he had all he could do just to hang on. The ezwal was doing nothing, apparently, to make it easier for his unwelcome rider. But after a time, when Jamieson accustomed himself better to the peculiar rhythm of a six-legged gallop, he began to feel exhilarated by this maddest of all wild rides. To the left, the jungle flashed by in a dizzying rush as the great animal raced along the strand. Then the trees closed overhead like an archway as it veered through an area less densely overgrown than the rest. Unerringly, the ezwal selected the route with no slackening of speed, as if a highly developed instinct were directing it back exactly the way it had come.

Suddenly there came a sharp command. "Hold tight!"

Jamieson instantly locked his grip on the harness and bent forward, bracing his feet hard against the straps just in time. Under him the steel muscles twisted. The great body whipped sideways; then with a tremendous surge it bounded forward.

Almost immediately the blinding flurry of speed diminished, and Jamieson was able to look back. He caught a glimpse of several large four-footed animals vaguely suggesting oversized hyenas, before they became obscured by the trees, hopelessly outdistanced. The beasts made no effort at pursuit. Very wise of them, it seemed to Jamieson. The magnificent creature under him, bigger than a dozen lions and deadlier than a hundred, was clearly well equipped for survival on this planet.

Jamieson's glow of honest admiration faded. His eyes had accidentally scanned above the trees and caught a movement in the sky. As he jerked his head up for a better look, a gray spaceship nosed out of the mists that plumed the skies of Eristan II.

A Rull warship!

In spite of himself, the recognition flashed clearly in

his mind. As he watched with speculative chagrin, the great ship, as cruel-looking as a swordfish with its finely pointed nose, sank toward the rim of the jungle ahead and disappeared. There was little doubt it was going to land. And no use trying to hide his surprise—it was too complete. The appearance of the great Rull ship was too potentially disastrous.

The ezwal's thought came with overtones of triumph. "I am aware of the thought in the back of your mind. Rather than be handed over to the Rull and have useful information extracted from your brain by force, you would destroy that brain with your own gun. I gather this sort of heroics is fairly common on both sides of the Rull-human conflict. I warn you: do not try to draw your gun. I'll smash you if you do."

Jamieson swallowed the hard lump in his throat. There was a sickness in him and a vast rage at the incredibly bad luck of the ship's coming here—now!

Miserable, he gave himself to the demanding rhythm of the ezwal's smooth gallop; and for a while there was only the odor-tainted wind, and the pad of six paws, a dull, flat flow of sound. Around them was the jungle, the occasional queer *lap, lap* of treacherous waters. And it was all there—the strangeness, the terribleness, of this wild ride of a man on the back of a blue-tinted beastlike being that hated him—and knew about the ship.

"You're crazy," he said at last in a flat voice, "if you believe the Rull mean any advantage to you or your kind." The theme was so familiar, and the truth of it too self-evident to him, that he had no trouble pursuing it with only the forepart of his attention. Meanwhile, he tensed his body ever so carefully, with his eyes casually on an outstretched limb just ahead. He summed up his argument with a vehemence that was quite genuine.

"The Rull are the most treacherous, racially self-centered—"

At the last instant, in gauging the distance for the hazardous leap, his purpose concerning that limb must have leaked from his mind. In a single convulsion of movement the ezwal reared and twisted; Jamieson was slammed forward against the metal-hard surface of a thrusting, mighty shoulder. Stunned, he fought blindly for balance and held on precariously as the animal turned and plunged his head and shoulders painfully. A moment later they emerged onto the beach of an emerald-green ocean bay. On the hard-packed, brown sand along the water's edge, the ezwal resumed its tireless, swift pace.

As if the incident just past were too trivial to discuss. it projected a casual thought. "I gathered from your mind that you think those creatures landed because they detected the minute energy discharge of the anti-gravity raft."

It took a while for Jamieson to recover his breath. He spoke at last, breathlessly, "There must be some logical reason, and unless you shut off the power as I did on the spaceship—"

The ezwal's thought was meditative. "That must be why they landed. If their instruments also registered your use of the gun on the snake, they also know some-one here is still alive. My best course, then, is to head straight for them before they find and attack us both as enemies."

"You're a fool!" said Jamieson with harsh emphasis. "They *will* kill us both as enemies. We *are* their enemies, and for but one reason: because we are not Rull. If you could understand that single point—"

"You would be expected to say that," the ezwal cut in sardonically. "Actually, I am somewhat indebted to them already. First, for the bolt of energy that twisted your ship and strained open one edge of my cage. Then for the distraction that enabled me to approach the crew of human beings undetected and destroy them all. I see no reason," the ezwal's thought concluded, "why the Rull would not welcome the offer I shall make on behalf of my own kind—to help them drive man from Carson's Planet. And it is to be hoped that the knowledge they take from your mind will contribute to that purpose."

Jamieson felt a black fury rising within him. He fought it down only because of the great urgency. He must not give up, even though the task seemed hopeless. He must convince this proud, unheeding ezwal of the utter folly of its plan. He held his voice to a grating monotone. "And when you have accomplished this, do you imagine that the Rull will quietly go away and leave you in peace?"

"Just let them dare remain!"

The sheer blind arrogance of this remark was almost too much. Again Jamieson fought to stem his anger. He must not forget, he told himself firmly, that this basically intelligent creature spoke from the relatively ignorant viewpoint of a nontechnological culture—and with no previous knowledge of mankind's archenemy. He spoke slowly, with great emphasis. "It's time you became aware of some facts. Man beat the Rull to Carson's Planet by a matter of a few months only. Even as you ezwals made it as difficult as you could for us to establish a base, we were fighting long, delaying actions in space, protecting you from the most ruthless, unreasonable beings the galaxy ever spawned. Man's best weapons are on a par with the Rull's best, but in some respects we've found they have the edge on us. For one thing, their technology is older, more evenly developed than ours. For another, they possess the amazing ability to alter and control certain electromagnetic waves, including the visible spectrum, with the cells of their bodies—an inheritance from the chameleonlike worms from which they are believed to have evolved. This faculty gives them a mastery of disguise and personal camouflage which has made their spy system a perpetual menace."

Jamieson paused, painfully conscious of the obstinate barrier between his own and the ezwal's minds. He went on doggedly. "We have *never* been able to dislodge the Rulls from any planet where they have become established. On the contrary, they drove us from three important bases, within a year of our first contact, before we fully realized the deadliness of the danger and resolved to stand firm everywhere, regardless of losses. And these are the beings you plan to ally yourself with, against Man?"

"In a very few minutes now—yes," came the ezwal's flintlike thought. The response was the more shocking because of its complete disregard of everything Jamieson had said.

"We are nearly there."

The time for argument was past. The realization came suddenly—so suddenly that Jamieson acted almost without conscious thought. Because of that circumstance, he was able to jerk out his blaster unsuspected and jam its muzzle hard against the ezwal's back. Triumphantly, he pressed the trigger; there was a blaze of white fire that passed unobstructed from the gun—and struck nothing!

A moment passed before he could grasp the startling fact that he was flying through the air, flung clear by a single, whiplike contortion of that great, supple body.

He struck brush. Bristling vines wrenched at his clothes, ripped his hands and tore savagely at the gun. His clothes shredded, blood came in red, ugly streaks—everything yielded to the clawing jungle but the one, all-important thing. With a bitter tenacity, he clung to the gun.

He landed on his side, rolled over in a flash and twisted up his gun, finger once more on the trigger. Three feet from that deadly muzzle, the ezwal drew up with a hideous snarl on its great square face, jumped thirty feet to one side and vanished among the tiers of matted foliage.

Dazed and trembling, almost ill, Jamieson sat up and surveyed the extent of his defeat, the limits of his victory.

III

CLOSE AROUND stood the curious, thick-boled trees of this alien jungle—curious because they were not really trees at all but mottled, yellow-brown fungi lifting with difficulty to a height of thirty or forty feet through the encumbering mass of thorn-studded vines, green lichens and bulbous, reddish grass. The ezwal had raged through other such dense wilderness with irresistible strength. For a man on foot—especially one who dared not waste the waning power of his gun—it was a nearly hopeless obstacle to any progress. The narrow strand of beach they had been traveling along was not too far, but it had veered off sharply in the wrong direction a short way back, and the ezwal had turned inland again.

One thing alone could be said for the present situation: at least he was not being borne helplessly along to a warship loaded with Rulls.

Rulls!

With a gasp, Jamieson leaped to his feet. There was a treacherous sagging of the matted grass under him, and he shuffled hastily to firmer ground; there he spoke swiftly in a low monotone, knowing that his thoughts, if not his sounds, would reach the keen intelligence lurking somewhere in that crazy quilt of light and shadow that enveloped him. "We've got to act fast. The discharges of my gun must have registered on Rull instruments, and they'll be here in minutes. This is your last chance to change your mind about the Rulls. I can only repeat that your scheme of enlisting the Rulls as allies is madness. Listen to the simple truth: Spy ships of ours lucky enough to return from their part of the galaxy have reported that every planet of the several hundred they have visited was inhabited by . . . Rulls. No other creatures of sufficient intelligence to offer organized resistance were to be found. There must have been some. *What happened to them?*"

Jamieson forced himself to pause, to let the question sink in, then went on rapidly. "Do you know what Man does when he encounters blind, fanatical hostility on any planet? It has happened a number of times. We quarantine the planet, at the same time throwing a cordon of ships around it to defend it from possible Rull attack. We then spend a great deal of time, which the Rulls would consider wasted, in attempting to establish peaceful relations with the planet's inhabitants. Teams of trained observers study their culture and infer as much as possible of their psychology, in order to get at the root of the trouble.

"If all attempts fail, we determine the most bloodless way of taking over their government or governments, and when this is accomplished we set about carefully revising their culture to remove from it only those elements, usually paranoid, which prevent cooperation with other races. After a generation, complete autonomy is restored and they are given the free choice of whether to join the federation which now includes nearly five thousand planets. Not once has this gigantic, expensive gamble on our part failed to pay off.

"I cite these examples merely to show you the vast gulf between the human way and the Rull way. There should be no need of our taking over Carson's Planet. You ezwals are intelligent enough to see who is your real enemy if you will open your minds. You yourself, here and now, can be the first."

There was no more to be said. He stood, then, and waited what seemed like a long time, but no faintest answering thought came from the strange, hushed wilderness about him. His shoulders slumped dejectedly. It was late afternoon, and he could see the blur of the sun through low-hanging vines. The hard realization came to him that his plight, already desperate, would soon get worse.

For even if he escaped the Rulls, in two hours at most the great fanged hunters and the reptilian flesh-eaters that roved the long nights of this primeval planet would emerge ravenous from their hideaways, their senses attuned to prey far better equipped to survive than he. Maybe if he could find a real tree with good strong, high-growing branches and rig up some warning system of vines . . .

He began to work forward, avoiding those clumps of dense brush which might conceal anything as large as an ezwal. It was rough going, and after a few hundred yards his arms and legs ached from the effort. At this point, quite abruptly, the first indication that the ezwal was still in the vicinity came to him in the form of a thought, sharp and urgent: "There is a creature hovering above me, watching me! It is like an enormous insect, as large as you, with diaphanous, amost invisible wings. I sense a brain, but the thoughts are . . . meaningless! I—"

"Not meaningless!" Jamieson cut in, his voice tense. "Alien is the word. The Rull is far more different from you and me than we are from each other. There is reason to think they may be from another galaxy, although this theory is unconfirmed. I don't wonder that you cannot read its mind."

As he spoke, Jamieson moved slowly into denser cover, holding his gun raised alertly. "Also, it is supported by an antigravity unit smaller and more efficient than any we human beings have been able to produce so far. What appears to be wings is only a sort of aura, an effect of its cellular control of light waves. You have the dangerous privilege of seeing a Rull in its natural form, which has been revealed to few human beings. The reason may be that it thinks you are a dumb beast, and you may be safe if— But no! It must be able to see the harness you are wearing!"

"No." There were overtones of distaste in the ezwal's denial. "I pulled the thing off right after we parted."

Jamieson nodded to himself. "Then *act* like a dumb beast. Snarl at it and sidle away but run like hell into the thickest underbrush if it reaches with one of its reticulate appendages toward any of those notches on either side of its body."

There was no answer.

The minutes dragged while Jamieson strained to catch sounds that might give a hint of the critical situation going on somewhere out of his sight. Would the ezwal make an attempt to communicate with the Rull by means other than telepathy, despite the danger which it seemed to realize? Worse yet, would the Rull, in becoming aware of the ezwal's intelligence, see an advantage in forming an unholy alliance? Jamieson shuddered to contemplate what might happen on Carson's Planet in that event.

He heard sounds—small, perturbing noises from all about: the distant crackle of undergrowth giving way to some large, unguessable body; faint snortings and grunts; an unearthly, pulsating low cry from some indeterminate point, possibly quite nearby. He burrowed deeper into the tangle of brush and peered out warily, half expecting some vast, menacing shape to form among the fetid mists now settling over the darkening ground.

The tension grew greater than he could bear. He *had* to know what was happening out there. Therefore, he would assume that the ezwal was acting on his advice.

With silent concentration, he projected a thought. "Is it still following you?"

The quick response surprised him. "Yes! It seems to be studying me. Stay where you are. I have a plan."

Jamieson sat bolt upright in his hideaway. "Yes?" he said.

The ezwal continued. "I will lead the creature to you. You will destroy it with your gun. In exchange, I offer to help you cross the Demon Straits."

Weariness slipped from Jamieson's shoulders. He straightened up and strode forward a few steps exultantly, momentarily unmindful of possible dangers.

There could be no doubt: the ezwal had abandoned all plans of an alliance with the Rulls! Whether this was because of Jamieson's explicit warnings or simply because of the ezwal's own discovery of the communication barrier made little difference. The important thing was that the threat which had come into being with the first sighting of the Rull ship was now ended.

It suddenly dawned on him that he was neglecting to accept the ezwal's proposal formally. He was about to do so when a wave of scathing thought from the giant beast made his response unnecessary.

"I sense your agreement, Trevor Jamieson, but take heed! I considered the Rull as an ally only in order that we might divest ourselves of our foremost enemy —Man! There was never any assurance that others of my race would have consented to an alliance of any kind. To many of us it would be unthinkable. Right now, I trust you are ready; I'll be there in seconds!"

Off to Jamieson's left there was sudden rending of brush. He tensed himself and as the sound grew louder raised his weapon expectantly. Through the mists, he caught sight of the ezwal, moving in a deceptively ponderous fashion on its six legs. At fifty feet, its three-in-line, steel-gray eyes were pools of light. And then as he searched the swirls of vapor over the beast's head for a dark, hovering shape—

"Too late!" came the ezwal's piercing thought. "Don't shoot; don't move! There are a dozen of them above me, and—"

A glaring white light burst silently over the scene, blanking out the flow from the ezwal's mind, then faded abruptly. With the after-image burning his eyes, Jamieson sank helplessly to a crouching posture, waiting for a doom that seemed certain.

Agonizing moments passed, and nothing happened. As his eyes partially regained their function, he could see what had saved him—no miracle, but only the fog, now rolling more thickly than ever. Distasteful though it was, it nevertheless concealed him as he cautiously worked his way back into the dense thicket and lay prone, peering out warily. Once or twice, through the obscuring mist, he glimpsed drifting shapes overhead. The absence of any wisp of thought from the ezwal was disturbing. Could that mighty beast have been struck dead so quickly and without an audible struggle?

It seemed unlikely. Energy in sufficient quantity for the purpose would not have been soundless. There was a more probable alternative: the Rulls must have worked a psychosis on the ezwal. Nothing else could explain that incoherent termination of thought in so powerful a mind.

Projective psychosis was used mainly on animals and other uncivilized and primitive life forms, unaccustomed to that sudden interplay of dazzling lights. And yet, in spite of its potent brain, the ezwal was very much animal, very much uncivilized and possibly extremely susceptible to mechanical hypnosis.

This line of reasoning would indicate that the Rulls had assumed that the ezwal *was* merely a primitive animal. Considering its appearance and deliberate behavior, this was a natural enough conclusion. Why, then, would they want to capture it alive? Perhaps they knew it was not native to this planet and were now seeking a clue as to its origin. Although this planet was within the periphery of human military bases, it was accessible enough to the Rulls that they could have visited here before.

Jamieson smiled bleakly. If the Rulls took the ezwal aboard their ship under the impression that it was an unintelligent animal, they could be in for a rude awakening when it regained its senses. The beast had wiped out a shipload of human beings who had been much closer to realizing its full potentialities.

A flicker of lightning lighted up the twilight sky to the north, and after a few seconds came the expected roll of thunder.

Jamieson sprang to his feet in abrupt excitement. No storm, that. It was man-made thunder, unmistakable to his ears—the vibrant roar of a broadside of hundred-inch battleship projectors.

A battleship! A capital ship, probably from the nearest base, on Kryptar IV, either on patrol or investigating energy discharges.

As he watched, there came another fleeting glare, and answering thunder closer but on a smaller scale. The Rull cruiser would be lucky if it got away!

But Jamieson's feeling of exultation dwindled quickly. This new turn of events could benefit him little, if at all. For him, there remained the night and its terrors. True, there would be no trouble now from the Rulls, but that was all. The running fight between the two ships would take them far into space and might last for days. Even if a patrol ship were sent here, and if he happened to see it, he had no way to signal it except with his gun—if there were any charge left in it by that time.

It was now so dark that his visibility was reduced to a very short distance, and his personal danger was thereby increased in geometric proportion. His eyes and his gun were his only safeguards: the former would very soon become nearly useless, while the small reserve of power in the latter had to be conserved for an indefinitely—perhaps impossibly—long time.

Uneasily, Jamieson peered into the gathering darkness around him. It was possible that he was already being stalked by some unseen monster. He started forward involuntarily, then checked himself. Panic would only invite disaster. He placed a finger in his mouth, held it up and felt a faint coolness on the right side of it. This direction was not too far from that in which he judged the antigravity raft might lie—but that was scarcely to be thought about now.

He started off upwind and promptly learned that progress through the jungle maze, difficult enough by day, was almost impossible by night. He could not retain any sense of direction and was obliged to recheck wind direction every few yards. It was now pitch-dark, and the continual stumbling over unseen obstacles made his passage so noisy that he debated the advisability of going on. But the alternative of remaining there immobile through the long hours of darkness seemed a thousand times worse. He blundered on, and a few moments later his fingers touched thick, carboniferous bark.

A tree!

IV

GREAT BEASTS stamped below as he clung to his precarious perch high above them. Eyes of fire glared at him. Seven times in the first few hours monstrous things clambered up the tree, mewing and slavering in feral desire and seven times his gun flashed a thinner beam of destroying energy. Great scale-armored carnivores whose approach shook the ground came to feed on the odorous flesh—and passed on.

Less than half the night gone! At this rate, the charge in his blaster would not last until morning—to say nothing of the next night, and the next, and the next. How many days would it take to reach the raft—providing he could find it at all? How many nights—how many *minutes* —could he survive after his weapon became useless?

The depressing thing was that the ezwal had just agreed to work with him against the Rulls. Victory so near, then instantly snatched afar. That thought ended. Because something, a horrible something, slobbered at the foot of the tree. Great claws rasped on bark, and then two eyes, disturbingly far apart, suddenly grew even farther apart, and he realized with sick terror that they were coming up at him with astounding speed.

Jamieson snatched at his gun, hesitated, then began to climb hastily up into the thinner branches. Every second, as he scrambled higher, he had the awful feeling that a branch would break and send him sliding toward the slavering thing below; and there was the more dreadful conviction that great jaws were at his heels.

His determination to save the power in his gun worked beyond his expectations. The beast was edging up into those thin branches after him when there was a hideous snarl below, and another, greater creature started up the tree. The fighting of animal against animal that started then was absolutely continuous. The tree shook as catlike beasts, with gleaming, hooked fangs, fought waddling, grunting shapes. Then, from the blackness nearby came a trumpeting scream, and a moment later a vast, long-necked monster, whose six-foot jaws might have reached Jamieson in his perch, lumbered into the carnage and attacked the whole struggling mass of killers indiscriminately. The first to die was dragged aside and eaten in an incredibly short time, after which the colossal creature wandered off, temporarily sated.

Toward dawn the continuous bellowing and snarling from near and far diminished, as stomach after eager stomach gorged itself and retired in enormous content to some cesspool of a lair.

At dawn he was still alive, completely weary, his body drooping with the desire for sleep, and in his mind was only the will to live, but no belief that he would survive the day. If only the ezwal had not cornered him so swiftly in the control room of the ship, he could have taken anti-sleep pills, fuel capsules for his gun, a compass chronometer, and—he smiled futilely at that line of reasoning—also a lifeboat which would by itself have enabled him to fly to safety.

At least there had been food capsules in the control room and he had snatched a month's supply. Jamieson descended the tree, put some distance between himself and the blood-soaked ground beneath it, and then took some nourishment.

He began to feel better. He began to think. As nearly as he could judge, based on an estimate of the ezwal's speed while they were traveling and the length of time, the raft should not be more than ten miles or so to the north. Barring a thousand accidents and perils, that would mean, for him, at least a full day or more of travel, depending on how many segments of sea and swamp lay between. Then, of course, he would have to beat the jungle in widening circles till he found the raft and charged his gun. The raft itself would be of no use; even with its power undepleted, it was only a sort of super-parachute, incapable of sustaining aloft much more than its own weight.

With a lot of luck, in other words, he would have the single advantage of a fully charged hand weapon with which to begin a hundred-mile trek to the wrecked ship. A hundred miles of jungle, sea and swamp . . . and the Demon Straits. A hundred miles of heat, humidity, carnivores—

But there was no point in dwelling on the depressing odds against him. One step at a time—that was the only way he could proceed and keep his sanity.

Bone-weary fram lack of sleep and the grueling tension of the night just past, he began the day's march. The first hour of struggling progress did little to hearten him. He had covered less than a mile, he was sure, and that was by no means in a straight line. He had wasted at least half of it in skirting areas of quagmire and several acre-wide bramble patches so thickly intertwined he doubted that even the ezwal could have penetrated them.

More time and energy had to be consumed in climbing an occasional tree in order to check on distance and direction—a vital matter, if he expected to arrive at the proper place from which to start a search for the raft.

By noon he estimated that he had advanced not more than three miles in the right direction. The white blur which marked the sun's position was now so close to the zenith as to make his bearings uncertain for the next hour or so. This fact, combined with the presence of a tall tree nearby and his physical exhaustion, made a compelling argument in favor of resting a while. There was a group of branches like an upreaching hand in the treetop; with some of the less abrasive vines in the vicinity he could tie himself in place and . . .

He awoke with the beasts of the Eristan night snarling their blood lust at the base of his tree.

His first reaction was terror—suffocating terror from the pressing, deadly darkness about him. Then, as he gradually regained control of his nerves, there came a strong feeling of chagrin at having lost so much time. But he had needed the rest desperately, he told himself, and there was no doubt that physically he felt much better. There was no way of telling how far into the night he had slept; he could only hope there was not too much of it left.

The tree vibrated suddenly as, far below, monstrous paws beat at its trunk. Startled, Jamieson began loosening the vines which secured him to his perch. Not that he could climb much higher, but he had learned that even a few feet could make all the difference.

No stars were visible through the heavy blanket of misty atmosphere which overlay this jungle planet; the absence of any means of marking the passage of time made the hours seem twice as long. Several times, ravening, catlike beasts essayed the climb to his perch, but only one came so close that Jamieson felt compelled to use his gun. When he did so, the thinness of its beam made his heart sink. But it worked, scorching the animal's forepaws and causing it to lose its grip. It fell, screaming and thrashing, to be fought over as a prize by the others below.

When at long last dawn came, it came slowly, and for some time Jamieson could not be sure the scene was actually lightening about him. The carnage had subsided below, and he could make out several of the hyena-like creatures encountered during his wild ride on the ezwal two days (only two days?) ago. They were feeding more or less quietly on the remains of an indeterminate number of dismembered carcasses. It had been the same the previous morning, but this time the sequel was different. For suddenly, silently, a huge head and forty feet of rounded body shot from the undergrowth like a massive javelin and struck the nearest scavenger, which shrieked once while being crushed to a pulp. The others scattered instantly and were gone.

The rest of the giant snake's body undulated leisurely from the tall grass, and it set about the business of swallowing its victim whole. The process took only a few minutes, but, afterward, the snake showed no disposition to move on. It lay there, while the bulge in its body elongated, gradually moving back and finally becoming almost unnoticeable. All this time Jamieson sat frozen in his perch, breathing as softly as possible. He had no extensive knowledge of the creature's hunting practices, but there seemed little doubt that it could pick him out of the treetop with ease, if it were to try.

After the longest hour of Jamieson's life, the snake stirred and slithered away. He waited a few minutes, then climbed down and followed in its clearly marked trail, moving as softly as possible and keeping a sharp lookout ahead. This would be the least likely quarter, he reasoned, from which the carrion-eaters would return to their feast, and he was counting on the snake not to double back or to stop very soon. After all, one animal was light fare for that colossal stomach, and the hunt must go on.

He was glad enough, however, to leave the trail after a few hundred yards and strike off in the approximate direction he had been traveling the day before. It was now full daylight, and the sun had probably risen, but it would not be visible until it was an hour or so high. That would be time enough to get his bearings and correct his course. In the meantime he would proceed in as straight a line as possible.

By noon he had penetrated considerably farther than on the previous day, due mainly to his improved physical condition. He allowed himself not more than an hour's rest and finished the last two miles by midafternoon. Weariness was settling heavily upon him now, but the thought of spending another endless night with a badly depleted weapon for protection spurred him to begin his circling search for the raft while a few hours of daylight remained.

There was a tall tree about fifty yards from where he stood, and he studied its structure intently for a minute, so that he would be able to recognize it from any angle. It would be his center point. His first circle would be at this distance, the second would be fifty yards farther out and so forth. This pattern would give him an excellent chance of spotting a large, metallic object like the raft, although some of the more densely overgrown areas would demand closer inspection. First of all, of course, he would climb the tree and see what might be seen from its top.

Four hours later he was tottering with exhaustion, having nearly completed his fifth round. It was growing dark. The preliminary survey from the tree had revealed nothing, and soon he must head back to it for another grueling night of fitful sleep and waking nightmares.

The thought spurred him on, as it had several times already. At least he would complete this round, despite the increasing danger of prowling beasts. But he no longer hid from himself the dull realization that he had been foolishly optimistic about finding the raft. He had learned one thing from his bird's-eye view that afternoon: the land was narrowing into a peninsula only a few miles across at this point. But to cover such an area at all thoroughly might take weeks.

He stumbled ahead, making no effort at moving quietly, actually little caring whether a final disaster ended this hopeless situation now or a few days from now.

The dense jungle fell away before him unexpectedly into a small clearing which had been invisible from the tree, only two hundred and fifty yards away. Even here, of course, the ground was not entirely bare but was thickly splotched toward the center with gray-colored creeping vines.

He had taken a few steps into the open when there was a movement of undergrowth on the far side, and a great shaggy beast with a fiery-eyed, maniacal face emerged to confront him, not fifty feet away. On sighting Jamieson, it growled hideously, opened its tusked jaws and broke into a full charge straight at him.

Jamieson froze, instinctively realizing the futility of attempting to run and waiting until the big animal gathered straightline momentum before trying to dodge.

It never did. It had hardly got under way when its legs became tangled in the gray vines, and it fell heavily among them. Incredibly, despite struggles that shook the ground, it seemed unable to get free. The reason was not immediately apparent, in the gathering darkness, but as Jamieson stared in fascination, he began to

see what was happening. The vinelike plant was alive
—ferociously alive! Tough, whiplike tendrils were wrap-
ping themselves about the beast's legs and neck faster
than its mighty efforts could break them apart. And
others, needle-tipped, were jabbing again and again
through the matted hair into its flesh. All at once the
great body stiffened with a jerk, its limbs extending
tautly to an unnatural, reaching position and remaining
so, motionless. The beast lay there as if turned to stone.

Now the vines slowed their frantic activity and began creeping up over the rigid carcass, spreading out
and gradually obscuring it from view.

Jamieson shook himself, tore his gaze from the horrid
spectacle and looked hastily about to make sure none
of the vines were growing close to him. He had identified the plant by now, although this was the first time
he had seen it or been aware of how it functioned. It
was the carnivorous Rytt plant, which together with
the giant snake species, made this planet unsuitable as
a military base. True, this creeping killer did not range
the entire planet, like the snake, but occurred only
where soil conditions were just right for its peculiar
metabolism. In such areas it generally abounded, and
Jamieson shuddered at the thought that he very possibly had passed fairly close to more than one patch
of it during the last several hours.

He was suddenly alarmed to notice how dark it had
become. At the same time he became aware that the
level of background noises which characterized this
primeval world had increased ominously in the last few
minutes. There was no such thing as a twilight hush
here; rather, it was a time of evil awakening, the stirring of ravening monsters from innumerable foul hideaways, the beginning of a protracted crescendo of wan-
ton slaughter.

He was in the act of turning toward the tree, whose

tip was just visible against the dimming sky, when he felt an amazing yet familiar probing at his mind, and a clear thought imposed itself there. "Not that way, Trevor Jamieson; the other way. The raft you are seeking is in the next clearing, not very far from the one you are in. And so am I, waiting for you. Once again, it seems, I need your help.

Jamieson stood still, trembling with both excitement and uncertainty. He had last seen the ezwal at the mercy of the Rulls. Could this be a Rull trick, and was the ezwal perhaps working with them, after all? But why would they bother to try to lure him—

"The Rulls who captured me are all dead," the ezwal cut in impatiently. "The lifeboat they landed in is also here, undamaged. I cannot operate it; therefore, I need your help. There are no beasts between you and it at the moment, so hurry!"

Jamieson turned eagerly and began to skirt the clearing, his energy suddenly renewed. The sketchy information grudgingly imparted by the ezwal was beginning to make some sense. The Rull warship must have been forced to leave so hastily there had not been time to pick up the scouting party it had sent out. And the latter group, thinking they had an unintelligent animal in their custody, had allowed the ezwal the chance it needed to wipe them out, as Jamieson had thought they might. So now—

"I did not kill them," came the ezwal's laconic thought. "It was not necessary. You will see in a moment what did."

Jamieson broke through a last fringe of spiked fern-like growth into a larger clearing. Along one side rested the hundred-foot, dark-metal Rull lifeboat, and on the other side lay the hard-sought raft, now rendered inconsequential by the turn of events. In between, amid gray splotches of Rytt plant, were the lifeless wormlike forms of a dozen Rulls, strange-appearing even in this alien environment. The gray creepers grew in profusion near the open door of the lifeboat, some extending even across the threshold into the dark interior, as if searching in their blind, instinctive way for more victims.

Jamieson blinked and guessed what had happened.

"Your logical processes are admirable," interposed the ezwal sardonically, "although a trifle slow. Yes, I am in the control room of the ship, with a closed steel door between myself and the creeping vines. I suggest that you use your gun to clear a path through them immediately and get inside the ship yourself. There are several beasts quite close, and you obviously cannot depend on the killer plant to protect you again."

Jamieson made a quick decision and turned toward the raft fifty feet away, giving the gray vines a wide berth. The raft itself was in the clear, fortunately; he climbed upon it and slid a cover plate aside, exposing the rather simple control mechanism. From his weapon he removed a screw cap and dropped a small capsule into his palm. This was the heart of his weapon; he would be completely helpless until it could be replaced.

He lifted the lid of a boxlike lead compartment in the control chamber, placed the capsule in a tiny, oddly shaped holder within it and closed the lid. That was all. In ten minutes a breeder reaction, initiated by the comparatively few neutrons left in the capsule, would bring it up to full charge. But he did not intend to wait that long. Three minutes, approximately, would produce all the charge he had to have.

Jamieson squatted there in the near-darkness, ready to try if need be to snatch the all-important capsule and get it back into the gun in time to save his life. He was by no means sure this could be done, but there was no help for it. The whole ugly situation was now quite clear in his mind. And the mere fact that no denial had come from the ezwal tended to prove it.

While he waited, looking constantly into the black shadows about the clearing, he spoke aloud, softly, but with grim emphasis. "So the Rulls didn't know about the Rytt plant. That is not too surprising; it is one of the few such types in the known galaxy. But they must have blundered into it at night for it to have got them all. Is that how it happened, or were you still in a trance at the time, like the stupid animal they thought you were?"

The ezwal's response was swift and haughty. "I threw off the hypnosis before they had finished floating me into the ship on the antigravity plate they had me chained to. With all of them present and armed, I thought it best not to show them how easily I could break loose, so I pretended to remain unconscious while they locked me in the storage hold. Then I broke the chains. I was waiting to see whether they would leave the ship again when there was a noise like thunder, and they all went outside. I could tell nothing from their strange thoughts except that they were excited. All at once they got even more excited, and then after a minute or so the thoughts stopped quite suddenly. I could guess what had happened, but to make sure, I broke out of the storage hold and looked out the main hatch. It was very dark by then, but I can see quite well in the dark. They were all dead."

Jamieson was wishing he could see that well in the dark. He fancied he saw something moving in one of the darker corners of the clearing, but he could not be sure. The three minutes must be nearly up by now. He would wait no longer. Forcing his trembling hands to move methodically, he took a small pair of tongs from their clip beside the lead box; opened the lid and carefully extracted the capsule. He inserted it in the gun, replaced the screw cap and breathed a deep sigh of relief.

He looked about the clearing once more, then stared into the suspected corner; there was nothing definite to be seen there yet. Probably only his imagination. But he continued to watch alertly as he stepped down from the raft and walked slowly toward the ship.

Again he spoke softly. "You have told me all I need to know. I think I can tell the rest of the story myself. After you saw that the Rulls were dead, you decided to spend the night in the ship. You would not trust your magnificent eyesight to protect you against all possible outcroppings of the Rytt plant. That is the one thing on this planet you truly fear. Your first encounter with it must have been an interesting one. In addition to your amazing speed and strength, I surmise that you needed a certain amount of luck to escape. And you found that the farther up the peninsula you went, the thicker it grew. You funked out completely. You decided you needed me—me and my gun. So you came back."

The first patch of gray creepers showed a little lighter against the dark ground. Jamieson pointed the gun downward, placed his other hand over his eyes and pressed the stud. There was a crackling roar as the searing beam of energy struck the ground, and though he could not see the brilliance of the flame, there was no doubt that the gun was adequately charged. He swung it from side to side as he walked forward several steps, then stopped, releasing the stud. He looked around and found that he could still see fairly well. He was standing in a wide black swath, and the next patch of gray was twenty feet ahead.

"You've been in that control room for two days, haven't you?" Jamieson went on. "It must have been a tight squeeze for you to get through the door. But you had to, because the main hatch operates by machinery which you don't understand and couldn't budge, for all your strength. The next morning when you opened the control-room door, you found the Rytt plant on the other side of it. I'll bet you closed it fast and threw all the clamps. That held back the plant, of course—its strength is not sufficiently concentrated to penetrate a hard metal door. It can clutch and stab you a hundred places at once, but it can't break down a steel door, as you can. So there you stayed."

The second patch of gray vines—a larger one—was dealt with like the first. Between Jamieson and the lifeboat now remained the largest, almost solid growth which enclosed the dead Rulls.

He talked on, in a quiet, edged tone. "For two days you have studied that control mechanism, trying to make sense out of it, and you have failed utterly. You must have reached the point where you were about to experiment blindly with the controls, no matter what happened. Then I showed up, and the situation changed. I am referring to my arrival in the vicinity, *hours ago.* You sensed that, of course. To you, it meant only a convenient alternative. You would continue to study the controls. If you couldn't figure them out before dark you would summon me, since I might not survive another night in my exhausted condition. But if you could possibly learn how to operate the ship, you would simply take off, leaving me here to die."

He paused and waited briefly, but there was still no response whatever from the ezwal, even to the final damning accusation. He was not surprised. The strange, proud creature in the ship must know full well that it could gain nothing by denial, and it was incapable of remorse.

Jamieson had now burned his way to within a few

feet of the lifeboat's main hatch. Only those creepers which extended into the ship were left. He set the intensity of his gun a few notches lower, to avoid damage to the sealing material which lined the hatch. He then spoke what he hoped would be his final words to this particular ezwal. "I'm going to burn away the creepers all the way to your door. When I do, you are to come out of there and go to the storage hold, where you are to stay. To see that you do, I'm going to set up this blaster so that a photoelectric relay will make it sweep the passageway if you so much as set foot in it. If you stay put, you won't be harmed. It will take two weeks to reach the nearest base, and from there we can head for Carson's Planet, where I will be very glad to turn you loose. In the meantime, you may find something edible in the storage room, though I doubt it. You can console yourself with the thought that, without any previous knowledge of astrogation or hyperdrive, you would undoubtedly have starved to death before you could get home by yourself. In any case, you should still be alive by the time I see the last of you.

"You have lost in the attempt to keep ezwal intelligence a secret from my government. But I shall have to report that in my opinion the average adult ezwal is just as impossible to reason with as if he were a dumb beast! And now you had better get your backside as far away from that door as you can. It's going to be hot in a minute!"

V

Two DAYS OUT from Eristan II, Jamieson made a radio contact with a cruiser of a race friendly to man. He explained his situation and asked that the ship let him use its powerful transmitters as a relay for him to contact the nearest Earth base. This was done.

But a week passed before an Earth battleship took aboard the Rull lifeboat and agreed to transport Jamieson and the ezwal to Carson's Planet. The commander of the battleship knew nothing of the ezwal situation. He merely verified Jamieson's identification of himself and accepted that he was an authorized personnel for ezwals.

When they arrived at Carson's Planet, Jamieson received permission from the base commander to have the battleship land in an area which was uninhabited by human beings. There he had his final conversation with the ezwal.

It was a beautiful setting. Rolling hills stretched into the northern reaches. To the west was a green forest, and in the valley to the south, the sparkle of a great river. Carson's Planet was a world of green abundance and water in plenty.

The ezwal trotted easily down to the ground, turned and looked up at Jamieson—who remained in an outjut of platform from the lower surface of the ship.

Jamieson began: "Have you changed your mind in any way?"

47

The ezwal replied, a curt thought, "Get off our planet and take all human beings with you!"

Jamieson said, "Will you tell your fellow ezwals that we will do this if they will develop a machine civilization that can defend the planet from the Rulls?"

"Ezwals will never agree to be slaves to machines." There was so much determination in the thought that Jamieson nodded his acceptance of the other's reality. Adult ezwals were emotionally set in a pattern that was probably millions of years in the making. The trap they were in was one from which they could not escape without assistance.

He said mildly, "Still, you're an individual. You want life for yourself as an entity. We proved that on Eristan II."

The ezwal seemed irritated and puzzled. "I gather from your mind that there are races which have a collective existence. The ezwals are separate beings who share a common goal. I sense, without clearly understanding your thought, that you regard this sepateness as a weakness."

"Not weakness," said Jamieson. "Just a point of attack. If you were a collective group, our approach would be different. For instance, you don't have a name, do you?"

The ezwal's thought showed disgust. "Telepaths recognize each other without needing such an elementary means of identification, and I warn you—" anger came into the thought—"if you think you will make conformists of ezwals by the idea I detect in your mind, you are hopelessly mistaken." Again the tenor of thought changed. The anger yielded to contempt. "But of course your problem is not what will you do with us but how will you convince your fellow human beings that ezwals are intelligent. I leave you with this problem, Trevor Jamieson."

The ezwal turned and trotted away across the grass. Jamieson called after it. "Thanks for saving my life, and thank you for proving again the value of cooperation against a common danger."

"I cannot," came the answer, "honestly offer thanks to a human being, for any reason whatsoever. Goodbye, and don't bother me any more."

"Goodbye," said Jamieson softly. He had a keen sense of regret and failure as the platform on which he stood began to roll back into the interior of the ship. As it clicked into position, he felt the antigravity effect as the great ship began to lift. Within seconds, it was accelerating.

Before leaving Carson's Planet, Jamieson spoke to the ruling military council. His suggestions received a formidably cold reception. As soon as his purpose was clear, the governor of the council interrupted him. "Mr. Jamieson, there is not a human being in this room or on this planet who has not suffered the death of a family member, murdered by these monstrous ezwals."

Since the remark was scientifically and militarily irrelevant, Jamieson waited. The governor continued. "If we were to believe that these creatures are intelligent, our impulse would be to exterminate them. For once, sir, Man should have no mercy for another race, and don't expect any mercy for ezwals from the inhabitants of this planet."

There was an angry murmur of approval from the other members of the council. Jamieson glanced around that circle of hostile faces and realized that Carson's Planet was indeed a precariously held base. Only a few times in history had man found an alien race so completely antipathetic as was the ezwal. What made the problem deadly was that Carson's Planet was one of the three bases on which human beings based their defense of the galaxy. Under no circumstances could there be a withdrawal. And if necessary, an extermination policy could be justified to the convention of Alien races allied to Man.

But even the key to extermination was his knowledge, and his alone—that ezwals communicated by telepathy. As beasts, ezwals had foiled all attempts to destroy them, by one simple reality. Few people had ever seen an ezwal, and the reason was now obvious—they always had advance warning.

If he told these hate-filled people that ezwals were telepaths, human scientists on Carson's Planet would quickly devise methods of destruction. These methods, based on mechanically created mind waves, would be designed to confuse the ezwal race, the members of which were actually quite naïve and vulnerable.

Standing there, Jamieson realized that this was not the time to tell about his experiences on Eristan II. Let them believe that he merely had a theory. Because of his position, most of them would believe his facts if he presented them. But they could all reject a mere theory on the grounds that they were on the scene, had tried everything, and he was merely passing by. And yet, he would have to make it clear that their rigid attitude was not acceptable.

"Gentlemen," said Jamieson, "and ladies—" he bowed to the three women members—"I cannot adequately express the sympathy and good will which motivated the Galactic Convention to send me here originally, in the hope that I might somehow help the people of Carson's Planet to resolve the ezwal problem. But I should tell you that I plan to recommend to the Convention that a plebiscite be held, the purpose of this plebiscite: to determine if the human race here will permit a rational solution to the ezwal problem."

The governor said coldly, "I think we are entitled to regard what you have just said as an insult."

Jamieson replied, "It was not intended as such. But my feeling is that the members of this council are so burdened with grief that we have no recourse but to go to the people. Thank you for listening to me."

Jamieson sat down. The State dinner that followed was eaten in almost complete silence.

After the dinner the vice-president of the council came over to Jamieson accompanied by a young woman. She seemed to be in her early thirties and she had blue eyes and a good-looking face and figure, but there was an unfeminine firmness in her expression that detracted from what would otherwise have been great beauty.

The man was barely polite as he said, "Mrs. Whitman has asked me to introduce her to you, Dr. Jamieson."

He performed the introduction quickly and walked off, as if the brief contact was all he could tolerate. Jamieson studied the woman thoughtfully. He recalled now that he had noticed her in serious conversation with first one, then the other of her two table companions—one of whom had been the man who had made the introduction.

She said now, "You're a doctor of science, aren't you?"

He nodded. "My Ph.D. is in physics, but it includes celestial mechanics and interstellar exploration—a highly specialized subject."

"I'm sure it is," she said. "I'm a widow with one child. My husband was a chemical engineer. I always marveled at the range of his knowledge." She added, as if it were an afterthought, "He was killed by an ezwal."

Jamieson guessed that the man must have been a top-ranking chemical engineer for his wife to be moving in council circles. But all he said was "I'm sorry for you and the child."

She stiffened at his sympathy, then relented. "The

51

reason I asked to be introduced to you is that most of the basic decisions about Carson's Planet were made two generations ago. I'd like you to stay over for a few days and I personally would like to show you what might be an alternative solution to the terrible problem we have here. We have a habitable moon—did you know that?"

Jamieson had noticed the moon as his ship came in. He said slowly, "You're implying it should be the base?"

"You could look at it," she said. "No one has for fifty years."

It was a point, he had to admit. In this vast galactic society, the attention span of individuals and even great organizations tended to be small. Basic data was often filed away and forgotten. There were always too many current problems waiting for an authority to give his attention to them. Every problem required a sustained look, and once that look was taken, and the decision made, the decision maker was reluctant to re-examine the data.

He doubted that she actually had a solution. But the immense antagonism of everyone had oppressed him, and so he warmed to her for actually communicating with him instead of hating him.

"Please come," she urged.

Jamieson mentally calculated his time situation. It would be some weeks yet before the "slow" freighter with the ezwal mother and her cub completed the thousands of light-years journey to Earth. He could easily take a few days and still reach Earth before the freighter.

"All right," he said, "I'll do it." He added, "Did I understand that you will be my guide?"

She laughed, showing her gleaming white teeth. "You don't think anyone else will even talk to you, do you?"

Ruefully, Jamieson saw her point.

VI

His eyes ached. He kept blinking them as he flew, striving to keep in sight the glitter of hurtling metal that was the power-driven spacesuit of his guide.

Already he regretted keenly making the trip to this strange moon of Carson's Planet. En route from the planet to the moon, in a great battleship he had commandeered, he had studied the Interstellar Encyclopedia, and there were stark facts. There were enormous temperature changes from day to night. Such planetary bodies simply could not be used to support the millions of people needed to back up a major military base.

The woman was desperately hard to see against the blazing brilliance of the sun, rising higher and higher from the fantastic horizon of Carson's Satellite. It was almost, Jamieson told himself, as if his guide were deliberately holding herself into the glare of the morning sun to distract his wearying mind and dull his strength.

More than a mile below, a scatter of forest spread unevenly over a grim, forbidding land. Pock-marked rock, tortured gravel and occasionally a sparse, reluctant growth of grass that showed as brown and uninviting as the bare straggle of forest—and was gone into distance as they sped far above, two shining things of metal, darting along with the speed of shooting stars.

Several times he saw herds of the tall, dapple-gray grass-eaters below; and once, far to the left, he caught the sheeny glint of a scale-armored, bloodsucker gryb.

It was hard to see his speedometer, which was built into the transparent headpiece of his flying space armor—hard because he had on a second headpiece underneath, attached to his electrically heated clothes; and the light from the sun split dazzlingly through the two barriers. But now that his suspicions were aroused, he strained his eyes against that glare until they watered and blurred. What he saw tightened his jaw into a thin, hard line. He snapped into his communicators; his voice was as cold and hard as his thoughts. "Hello, Mrs. Whitman."

"Yes, Doctor Jamieson!" The woman's voice sounded in his communicators; and it seemed to Jamieson's alert hearing that the accent on the "Doctor" held the faintest suggestion of a sneer and a definite hostility. "What is it, Doctor?"

"You told me this trip would be five hundred and twenty-one miles or—"

"Or thereabouts!" The reply was swift, but the hostility more apparent, more intentional.

Jamieson's eyes narrowed to steely gray slits. "You said five hundred and twenty-one miles. The figure is odd enough to be presumed exact, and there is no possibility that you would not know the exact distance from the Five Cities to the platinum mines. We have now traveled six hundred and twenty-nine miles—more every minute—since leaving the Five Cities over two hours ago, and—"

"So we have!" interrupted the young woman with unmistakable insolence. "Now isn't that too bad, Doctor Trevor Jamieson."

He was silent, examining the situation for its potential menace. His first indignant impulse was to pursue the unexpected arrogance of the other, but his brain, suddenly crystal-clear, throttled the desire and leaped ahead in a blaze of speculation.

There was murderous intent here. His mind ticked coldly, with a sense of something repeated, for the threat of death he had faced before, during all the tremendous years when he had roamed the farthest planets. It was icily comforting to remember that he had conquered in the past. In murder, as in everything else, experience counted.

Jamieson began to decelerate against the fury of built-up velocity. It would take time—but perhaps there still was time, though the other's attitude suggested the crisis was dangerously near. There was no more he could do till he had slowed considerably.

Jamieson quieted his leaping pulses and said gently, "Tell me, is the whole council in on this murder? Or is it a scheme of your own?"

"There's no harm in telling you now," the woman retorted. "We decided you're not going to make any such recommendation about ezwals to the Galactic Convention. Of course we knew this moon would never be accepted as a substitute base."

Jamieson laughed, a hard, humorless but understanding laugh that hid the slow caution with which he slanted toward the ground. The strain of the curving dive racked his body, tore at his lungs, but he held to it grimly. He was alone in the sky now; the shining spacesuit of his guide had vanished into the dim distance. Evidently she had not turned her head or noticed the deviation on her finder. Anxious for the discovery to be as long delayed as possible, Jamieson said, "And how are you going to kill me?"

"In about ten seconds," she began tautly, "your engine—" She broke off. "Oh, you're not behind me any more. So you're trying to land. Well, it won't do you any good. I'll be right back that way—"

Jamieson was only fifty feet from the bleak rock when there was a sudden grinding in the hitherto silent mechanism of his motor. The deadly swiftness of what happened then left no time for more than instinctive action. He felt a pain against his legs, a sharp, tearing pain, a dizzy, burning sensation that staggered his reason. Then he struck the ground, and with a wild, automatic motion jerked off the power that was being so horribly short-circuited, that was burning him alive. Darkness closed over his brain like an engulfing blanket.

The blurred world of rock swaying and swirling about him—that was Jamieson's awakening! He forced himself to consciousness and realized after a moment of mental blankness that he was no longer in his spacesuit. And when he opened his eyes he could see without a sense of dazzle, now that he had only the one helmet—the one attached to his electrically heated clothes. He grew aware of something—an edge of rock—pressing painfully into his back. Dizzily, but with sane eyes, he looked up at the determined young woman who was kneeling beside him. She returned his gaze with unsmiling hostility and said curtly, "You're lucky to be alive. Obviously you shut off the motor just in time. It was being shorted by lead grit and burned your legs a little. I've put some salve on, so you won't feel any pain; and you'll be able to walk."

She stopped and climbed to her feet. Jamieson shook his head to clear away the black spots and then gazed up at her questioningly, but he said nothing. She seemed to realize what was on his mind. "I didn't think I'd be squeamish with so much at stake," she confessed almost angrily, "but I am. I came back to kill you, but I wouldn't kill even a dog without giving him a chance. Well, you've got your chance, if it's worth anything."

Jamieson sat up. His eyes narrowed on her face inside her helmet. He had met hard women before but never anyone who seemed more sincere and honest about her intentions, now that she was out in the open.

Frowning with thought, Jamieson looked around; and his eyes, trained for detail, saw a lack in the picture.

"Where's your spacesuit?"

The woman nodded her head skyward. Her voice held no quality of friendliness as she said, "If your eyes are good, you'll see a dark spot, almost invisible now, to the right of the sun. I chained your suit to mine, then gave mine power. They'll be falling into the sun about three hundred hours from now."

He pondered that matter-of-factly. "You'll pardon me if I don't quite believe that you've decided to stay and die with me. I know that people will die for what they believe to be right. But I can't quite follow the logic of why you should die. No doubt you have made arrangements to be rescued."

The woman flushed, her growing dark with the turgid wave of angry color. "There'll be no rescue," she said. "I'm going to prove to you that, in this matter, no individual in our community thinks of himself or herself. I'm going to die here with you because, naturally, we'll never reach the Five Cities on foot, and as for the platinum mines, they're even farther away."

"Pure bravado!" Jamieson said. "In the first place your staying with me proves nothing but that you're a fool; in the second, I am incapable of admiring such an action. However, I'm glad you're here with me, and I appreciate the salve on those burns."

Jamieson climbed gingerly to his feet, testing his legs, first the right, then the left, and felt a little sickening surge of dizziness that he fought back with an effort. "Hm-m-m," he commented aloud in the same matter-of-fact manner as before. "No pain, but weak. That salve ought to have healed the burns by dark."

"You take it very calmly," said Barbara Whitman acridly.

He nodded. "I'm always glad to realize I'm alive and

I feel that I can convince you that the course which I plan to recommend for Carson's Planet is a wise solution."

She laughed harshly. "You don't seem to realize our predicament. We're at least twelve days from civilization—that's figuring sixty miles a day, which is hardly possible. Tonight the temperature will fall to a hundred below freezing, at least, though it varies down to as low as a hundred and seventy-five below, depending on the shifting of the satellite core, which is very hot, you know, and very close to the surface at times. That's why human beings—and other life—can exist on this moon at all. The core is jockeyed around by the Sun and Carson's Planet, with the Sun dominating, so that it's always fairly warm in the daytime and why also, when the pull is on the other side of the planet, it's so devilish cold at night. I'm explaining this to you so you'll have an idea of what it's all about."

"Go on," Jamieson said without comment.

"Well, if the cold doesn't kill us, we're bound to run into at least one bloodsucker gryb every few days. They can smell human blood at an astounding distance, and blood, for some chemical reason, drives them mad with hunger. Once they corner a human being it's all up. They tear down the largest trees or dig into caves through solid rock. The only protection is an atomic blaster, and ours went up with our suits. We've got only my hunting knife. Besides all that, our only possible food is the giant grass-eater, which runs like a deer at the first sight of anything living and which, besides, could kill a dozen unarmed men if it were cornered. You'll be surprised how hungry it is possible to get within a short time. Something in the air—and, of course, we're breathing filtered air—speeds up normal digestion. We'll be starving to death in a couple of hours."

"It seems to give you a sort of mournful satisfaction," Jamieson said dryly.

She flashed, "I'm here to see that you don't get back alive to the settlement, that's all."

Jamieson scarcely heard her. His face was screwed into a black frown. "I'm sorry that you came back. I regret keenly that a woman is in such a dangerous situation. Your friends are scoundrels to have permitted it. But I'll get back safely."

She laughed contemptuously. "Impossible. You try living off the soil of this barren moon; try killing a gryb with your bare hands."

"Not my hands," replied Jamieson grimly. "My brains and my experience. We're going to get back to the Five Cities in spite of these natural obstacles, in spite of you!"

In the silence that followed, Jamieson examined their surroundings. He felt his first real chill of doubt as his eyes and mind took in that wild and desolate hell of rock that stretched to every horizon. No, not every! Barely visible in the remote distance of the direction they would have to go was a dark mist of black cliff. It seemed to swim there against the haze of semi-blackness that was the sky beyond the horizon. In the near distance the piling rock showed fantastic shapes, as if frozen in a state of writhing anguish. And there was no beauty in it, no sweep of grandeur, simply endless, desperate miles of black, tortured *deadness*—and silence!

He grew aware of the silence with a start that pierced his body like a physical shock. The silence seemed suddenly alive. It pressed unrelentingly down upon that flat stretch of rock where they stood. A malevolent silence that kept on and on, without echoes, without even a wind now to whistle and moan over the billion caves and gouged trenches that honeycombed the bleak, dark, treacherous land around them. A silence that seemed the very spirit of this harsh and deadly little world, here under that cold, brilliant sun.

"Oppressive isn't it?"

Jamieson stared at her without exactly seeing her. His gaze was far away. "Yes," he said thoughtfully. "I'd forgotten what it felt like; and I hadn't realized how much I'd forgotten. Well, we'd better get started."

As they leaped cautiously over the rock, assisted by the smaller gravitation of the moon, the woman said, "What do you think you've found out about ezwals?"

"I can't tell you that," Jamieson replied. "If you knew what I know, hating them, you'd destroy them."

"Why didn't you tell the council you had specific information instead of merely offering what seemed to be a hypothesis? They're sensible people."

"Sensible!" echoed Jamieson, and his tone of voice was significant with irony.

"I don't believe you have anything but a theory," said Barbara Whitman flatly. "So stop pretending."

VII

TWO HOURS LATER the sun was high in those dark, gloomy heavens. It had been two hours of silence; two hours while they tramped precariously along thin stretches of rock between fantastic valleys that yawned on either side, while they skirted the edge of caves whose bleak depths sheered straight down into the restless bowels of the moon; two hours of desolation.

The great black cliff, no longer misted by distance, loomed near and gigantic. As far as the eye could see it stretched to either side, and from where Jamieson toiled and leaped ever more wearily, its wall seemed to rear up abrupt and glassy and unscalable.

He gasped, "I hate to confess it, but I'm not sure I can climb that cliff."

The woman turned a face toward him that had lost its brown healthiness in a gray, dull fatigue. A hint of fire came into her eyes. "It's hunger!" she said curtly. "I told you what it would be like. We're starving."

Jamieson pressed on, but after a moment slackened his pace and said, "This grass-eater—it also eats the smaller branches of trees, doesn't it?"

"Yes. That's what its long neck is for. What about it?"

"Is that all it eats?"

"That and grass."

"Nothing else?" Jamieson's voice was sharp with question, his face drawn tight with insistence. "Think."

Barbara bridled. "Don't take that tone to me," she said. "What's the use of all this anyway?"

"Sorry—about the tone, I mean. What does it drink?"

"It likes ice. They always stay near the rivers. During the brief melting periods each year, all the water from the forests runs into the rivers and freezes. The only thing it eats or drinks is salt. Like so many animals, they absolutely have to have salt, and it's pretty rare."

"Salt! That's it!" Jamieson's voice was triumphant. "We'll have to turn back. We passed a stretch of rock salt about a mile back. We'll have to get some."

"Go back! Are you crazy?"

Jamieson stared at her, his eyes gray pools of steely glitter. "Listen, Barbara, I said a while ago that I didn't think I could climb those cliffs. Well, don't worry, I'll climb them. And I'll last through all today, and all tomorrow and the other twelve or fifteen or twenty days. I've put on about twenty-five pounds during the last ten years that I've been an administrator. Well, damn it, my body'll use that as food, and by heaven, I'll be alive and moving and going strong—and I'll even carry you if necessary. But if we expect to kill a grass-eater and live decently, we've got to have salt. I saw some salt, and we can't take a chance on passing it up. So back we go."

They glared at each other with the wild, tempestuous anger of two people whose nerves are on ultimate edge. Then Barbara drew a deep breath and said, "I don't know what your plan is, but it sounds crazy to me. Have you ever seen a grass-eater? Well, it looks something like a giraffe, only it's bigger and faster on its feet. Maybe you've got some idea of tempting it with salt and then killing it with a knife. I tell you, you can't get near it, but I'll go back with you. It doesn't matter, because we're going to die, no matter what you think. What I'm hoping is that a gryb sees us. It'll be quick that way."

"There is something," said Jamieson, "pitiful and horrible about a beautiful woman who is determined to die."

"You don't think I want to die!" she flashed. Her passionate voice died abruptly, but Jamieson knew better than to let so much fierce feeling die unexplored.

"What about your child?"

He saw by the wretched look on her face that he had struck home. He felt no compunction. It was imperative that Barbara Whitman develop a desire to live. In the crisis that seemed all too near now, her assistance might easily be the difference between life and death.

It was odd, the fever of talk that came upon Jamieson as they laboriously retraced their steps to the salt rock. It was as if his tongue, as if all of his body, had become intoxicated; and yet his words, though swift, were not incoherent but reasoned and calculated to convince her. He spoke of the problems of Man landing on inhabited planets and of the many solutions that had been achieved by reason. Human beings often did not realize how deeply attached life was to its own planet and how desperately each race fought against intruders.

"Here's your salt!" Barbara interrupted him finally.

The salt rock composed a narrow ledge that protruded like a long fence which ran along in a startlingly straight line and ended abruptly at a canyon's edge, the fence rearing up, as if cringing back in frank dismay at finding itself teetering on the brink of an abyss.

Jamieson picked up two pieces of salt rubble and slipped them into the capacious pockets of his plainsmanlike coat—and started back toward the dark wall of cliff nearly three miles away. They trudged along in silence. Jamieson's body ached in every muscle, and every nerve pulsed alarms to his brain. He clung with a desperate, stubborn strength to each bit of rock projecting from the cliff wall, horribly aware that a slip meant death. Once he looked down, and his brain reeled in dismay from the depths that fell away behind him.

Through blurred vision he saw the woman's figure a few feet away, the tortured lines of her face a grim reminder of the hunger weakness that was corroding the very roots of their two preciously held lives.

"Hang on!" Jamieson gasped. "It's only a few more yards."

They made it and collapsed on the edge of that terrific cliff, too weary to climb the gentle slope that remained before they could look over the country beyond, too exhausted to do anything but lie there, sucking the life-giving air into their lungs. At last Barbara whispered, "What's the use? If we had any sense w'd jump off this cliff and get it over with."

"We can jump into a deep cave any time," Jamieson retorted. "Let's get going."

He rose shakily to his feet, took a few steps, then stiffened and flung himself down with a hissing intake of his breath. His fingers grabbed her leg and jerked her back brutally to a prone position.

"Down for your life. There's a herd of grass-eaters half a mile away. And they *mean* life for us."

Barbara crawled up beside him, almost eagerly; and the two peered cautiously over the knob of rock out onto a grassy plain. The plain was somewhat below them. To the left, a scant hundred yards away, like a wedge driven into the grassland, was the pointed edge of a forest. The grass beyond seemed almost like a projection of the forest growth. It, too, formed a wedge that petered out in bleak rock. At the far end of the grass was a herd of about a hundred grass-eaters.

"They're working this way!" Jamieson said. "And they'll pass close to that wedge of trees."

A faint air of irony edged his companion's voice as she said, "And what will you do—run out and put salt on their tails? I tell you, Doctor Jamieson, we haven't got a thing that—"

"Our first course," said Jamieson, unheeding, seeming to think out loud, "is to get into that thick belt of trees. We can do that by skirting along this cliff's edge and putting the trees between us and the animals. Then you can lend me your knife."

"Okay," she agreed in a tired voice. "If you won't listen, you'll have to learn from experience. I tell you, you won't get within a quarter of a mile of those things."

"I don't want to," Jamieson retorted. "You see, Barbara, if you had more confidence in *life,* you'd realize that this problem of killing animals by cunning has been

solved before. It's absolutely amazing how similarly it
has been solved on different worlds and under widely
differing conditions. One would almost suspect a common evolution, but actually it is only a parallel situation producing a parallel solution. Just watch me."

"I'm willing," she said. "There's almost any way I'd
rather die than by starving. A meal of cooked grass-eater
is tough going, but it'll be pure heaven. Don't forget,
though, that the bloodsucker grybs follow the grass-
eater herds, get as near as possible at night, then kill
them in the morning when they're frozen. Right now,
with darkness near, a gryb must be out there somewhere, hiding, sneaking nearer. Pretty soon he'll smell
us, and then he'll—"

"We'll come to the gryb when he comes for us," said
Jamieson calmly. "I'm sorry I never visited this moon
in my younger days; these problems would all have
been settled long ago. In the meantime, the forest is
our goal."

Jamieson's outer calmness was but a mask for his
inner excitement. His body shook with hunger and eagerness as they reached the safety of the forest. His fingers were trembling violently as he took her knife and
began to dig at the base of a great, bare, brown tree.

"It's the root, isn't it," he asked unsteadily, "that's
so tough and springy that it's almost like fine tem-
pered steel, and won't break even if it's bent into a circle?
They call it eurood on Earth, and it's used in industry."

"Yes," she said doubtfully. "What are you going to
do—make a bow? I suppose you could use a couple of
grass blades in place of catgut. The grass is pretty
strong and makes a good rope."

"No," said Jamieson. "I'm not making a bow and arrow. Mind you, I can shoot a pretty mean arrow. But
I'm remembering what you said about not being able to
get within a quarter of a mile of the beasts."

He jerked out a root, which was about an inch in thickness, cut off a generous two-foot length and began to sharpen, first one end, then the other. It was hard going, harder than he had expected, because the knife skidded along the surface almost as if it were metal. Finally it obtained a cutting hold. "Makes a good edge and point," he commented. "And now, give me a hand in bending this double, while I tie some grass blades around to keep it this way."

"O-oh!" she said wonderingly. "I see-e-e! That is clever. It'll make a mouthful about six inches in diameter. The grass-eater that gets it will gobble it up in one gulp to prevent any of the others getting the salt you're going to smear on it. His digestive juices will dissolve the grass string, the points will spring apart and tear the wall of his stomach, producing an internal hemorrhage."

"It's a method," said Jamieson, "used by the primitives of various planets, and our own Eskimo back on Earth uses it on wolves. Naturally, they all use different kinds of bait, but the principle is the same."

He made his way cautiously to the edge of the forest. From the shelter of a tree he flung the little piece of bent wood with all his strength. It landed in the grass a hundred and fifty feet away.

"We'd better make some more," Jamieson said. "We can't depend on one being found."

The eating was good; the cooked meat tough but tasty; and it was good, too, to feel the flow of strength into his body. He sighed at last and stood up, glanced at the sinking sun, an orange-sized ball of flame in the western sky.

"We'll have to carry sixty Earth pounds of meat apiece; that's four pounds a day for the next fifteen days. Eating meat alone is dangerous; we may go insane, though it really requires about a month for that.

We've got to carry the meat because we can't waste any more time killing grass-eaters."

Jamieson began to cut into the meaty part of the animal, which lay stretched out on the tough grass, and in a few minutes had tied together two light bundles. By braiding grass together, he made himself a pack sack and lifted the long shank of meat until it was strapped to his back. There was a little adjustment necessary to keep the weight from pressing his electrically heated clothes too tightly against him; when he looked up finally, he saw that Barbara was looking at him peculiarly.

"You realize, of course," she said, "that you're quite insane now. It's true that, with these heated suits, we may be able to live through the cold of tonight, provided we find a deep cave. But don't think for a second that, once a gryb gets on our trail, we'll be able to throw it a piece of sharpened wood and expect it to have an internal hemorrhage."

"Why not?" Jamieson asked, and his voice was sharp.

"Because it's the toughest creature ever spawned by a crazy evolution, the main reason I imagine why no intelligent form of life evolved on this moon. Its claws are literally diamond hard; its teeth can twist metals out of shape; its stomach wall can scarcely be cut with a knife, let alone with crudely pointed wood."

Her voice took on a note of exasperation. "I'm glad we've had this meal; starving wasn't my idea of a pleasant death. I want the quick death that the gryb will give us. But for heaven's sake, get it out of your head that we shall live through this. I tell you, the monster will follow us into any cave, cleverly enlarge it wherever he has difficulty, and he'll get us because eventually we'll reach a dead end. They're not normal caves, you know, but meteor holes, the result of a cosmic cataclysm millions of years ago, and they're all twisted out of shape by the movement of the planet's crust. As for tonight, we'd better get busy and find a deep cave with plenty of twists in it, and perhaps a place where we can block the air currents from coming in. The winds will be arriving about a half an hour before the sun goes down, and our electric heaters won't be worth anything against those freezing blasts. It might pay us to gather some of the dead wood lying around, so we can build a fire at the really cold part of the night."

Getting the wood into the cave was simple enough. They gathered great armfuls of it and tossed it down to where it formed a cluttered pile at the first twist in the tunnel. Then, having gathered all the loose wood in the vicinity, they lowered themselves down to the first level, Jamieson first in a gingerly fashion, the young woman—Jamieson noticed—with a snap and spring. A smile crinkled his lips. The spirit of youth, he reflected, would not be suppressed.

They were just finishing throwing the wood down to the next level when suddenly a shadow darkened the cave mouth. Jamieson glanced up with a terrible start and had a fleeting glimpse of great fanged jaws and glowing eyes that glared from a hideous head; a thick red tongue licked out in unholy desire, and a spray of saliva rained down upon their transparent metal helmets and leatherlike clothes.

And then Barbara's leather-covered hands bit like sharp stones into his arms; he felt himself dragged over the edge.

They landed unhurt among the loose pile of branches below and scrambled frantically to throw it farther down. A great mad clawing and horrible bass mewing above them whipped them to desperate speed. They made it just as that enormous head peered down from the second level, visible only by the phosphorescent glow of its eyes, like two burning coals a foot and a half apart.

There was a terrific scrambling sound behind them as they pushed wildly down to the next level; a rock bounced down, narrowly missing them as it clattered past; and then, abruptly, silence and continuing darkness.

"What's happened?" Jamieson asked in bewilderment.

There was bitterness in her voice as she replied, "It's wedged itself in, because it's realized it can't get us in the few minutes left before it freezes for the night; and, of course, now we won't be able to get out past it, with that great body squeezed against the rock sides. It's really a very clever animal in its way. It never chases grass-eaters but just follows them. It has discovered that it wakes up a few minutes before they do; naturally, it thinks we, too, will freeze and that it will wake up before we will. In any event, it knows we can't get out. And we can't. We're finished."

All that long night Jamieson waited and watched. There were times when he dozed, and there were times when he thought he was dozing, only to realize with a dreadful start that the horrible darkness had played devil's tricks on his mind.

The darkness during the early part of the night was like a weight that held them down. Not the faintest glimmer of natural light penetrated that Stygian night. And when, at last, they made a fire from their pile of brush, the pale, flickering flames pushed but feebly against the pressing, relentless force of the darkness and seemed helpless against the cold.

Jamieson began to notice the cold, first as an uncomfortable chill that ate into his flesh, and then as a steady, almost painful, clamminess that struck into his very bones. The cold was noticeable, too, in the way white hoarfrost thickened on the walls. Great cracks appeared in the rock; and not once but several times sections of the ceiling collapsed with a roar that threatened their lives. The first clatter of falling debris seemed to waken the woman from a state of semicoma. She staggered to her feet; and Jamieson watched her silently as she paced restlessly to and fro, clapping her gloved, heated hands together to keep them warm.

"Why not," Jamieson asked, "go up and build a fire against the gryb's body? If we could burn him—"

"He'd just wake up," she said tersely, "and besides, his hide won't burn at ordinary temperatures. It has all the properties of metallic asbestos—conducts heat but is practically noncumbustible."

Jamieson was silent, frowning; then he said, "The toughness of this creature is no joke—and the worst of it all is that our danger, the whole affair, has been utterly useless. I'm the only person who has a solution to the ezwal problem, and I'm the one you're trying to kill."

"I don't really suppose it matters," she said. "What's the use of you and I arguing on this subject? It's too late. In a few hours that damn thing that's got us sealed in here will wake up and finish us. There's nothing we've got that can hold it back one inch or one second."

"Don't be so sure of that!" Jamieson said. "I admit the toughness of this monster has me worried, but don't forget what I've said: these problems have been solved before on other planets."

"You're mad! Even with a blaster, it's touch and go getting the gryb before it gets you. Its hide is so tough it won't begin to disintegrate until your heart's in your boots. What can we do against a thing like that when all we've got is a knife?"

"Let me have the knife," Jamieson replied. "I want to sharpen it." His face twisted into a wry smile. Perhaps it didn't mean much, but there was a tone of acceptance of him in her voice.

The sustained darkness of that night, the insistent crackle of the palely flickering fire seemed to become more and more alive as the nervous hours twitched by. It was Jamieson who was pacing now, his powerful body restless and tense with anxious uncertainty.

It was getting distinctly warmer; the white hoarfrost was melting in places, yielding for the first time to the heat of the spluttering flame; and the chill was no longer reaching clammily through his heated clothes.

A scatter of fine ashes lay on the ground, indicating how completely the fuel had burned away; but even as it was, the cave was beginning to show a haze of smoke fumes, through which it was difficult to see properly.

Abruptly there was a great stirring above them, and then a deep, eager mewing and a scrambling, scratching sound. Barbara Whitman jerked erect from where she had been lying. "It's awake," she gasped, "and it's remembered."

"Well," said Jamieson grimly, "this is what you've been longing for."

From across the fire, she stared at him moodily. "I'm beginning to see that killing you will solve nothing. It was a mad scheme."

A rock bounded down and crashed between them, missing the fire, then vanishing noisily into the darkness beyond. There followed a horrible squeezing, a rasping sound as of brittle scales scraping rock, and then, terribly near, the drumming sound as of a monstrous sledge hammer at work.

"He's breaking off a piece of rock!" she said breathlessly. "Quick! Get into a concavity against the wall. Those rocks may come tumbling down here, and they won't miss us forever. What are you doing?"

"I'm afraid," said Jamieson in a shaky voice, "I've got to risk the rock. There's no time to waste."

His leather-covered hands trembled with the excitement that gripped him as he hastily unfastened one of the glove extensions. He winced a little as his hand emerged into the open air and immediately jerked it over the hot flame of the fire.

"Phew, it's cold. Must still be ninety below. I'll have to warm this knife or it'll stick to my skin."

He held the blade into the flame, finally withdrew it, made a neat incision in the thumb of his bare hand and wiped the blood onto the knife blade, smearing it on until his hand, blue with the cold, refused to bleed any more. Then he quickly slipped it back into his glove. It tingled as it warmed, but in spite of the pain he picked up a flaming faggot by its unburned end and walked along into the darkness, his eyes searching the floor. He was vaguely aware of the woman following him.

"Ah," said Jamieson, and even in his own ears his voice sounded wrenched from him. He knelt quiveringly beside a thin crack in the rock. "This'll be just about right. It's practically against the wall, protected from falling rocks by this projecting edge of wall." He glanced up at the woman. "The reason I had us camp here last night instead of farther down was because this ledge is nearly sixty feet long. The gryb is about thirty feet long from tail to snout, isn't it?"

"Yes."

"Well, this will give it room to come down and walk a few feet; and besides, the cave is wide enough here for us to squeeze past it when it's dead."

"When it's dead!" she echoed with a faint moan. "You must be the world's prize fool!"

Jamieson scarcely heard her. He was carefully inserting the handle of the knife into the crack of the rock, wedging it in. He tested it.

"Hm-m-m, it seems solid enough. But we'll have to make doubly sure."

"Hurry," Barbara exclaimed. "We've got to get down to the next level. There's just a chance that there is a connection somewhere below with another cave."

"There isn't! I went down to investigate while you were sleeping. There are only two more levels after this."

"For heaven's sake, it'll be here in a minute."

"A minute is all I need," Jamieson replied, struggling to calm his clamoring heart, to slow the convulsive gasping of his lungs. "I want to pound these slivers of rock beside the knife to brace it."

And Jamieson pounded while she danced frantically from one foot to another in a panic of anxiety. He pounded while that scrambling from above became a roaring confusion, so near now that it was deafening. He pounded while his nerves jangled and shook from the hellish bass mewing that blasted down from the ravenous beast.

And then, with a gasp, he flung aside the piece of rock with which he had been hammering, and they lowered themselves recklessly over the edge—just as two great glowing eyes peered down upon them. The firelight revealed the vague outlines of a dark, fanged mouth, a thick, twisting tongue; and then there was a scaly glitter as the monstrosity plunged downward right onto the fire.

Jamieson saw no more. He let go his hold and skittered downward for nearly twenty feet before he struck bottom. For a minute he lay there, too dizzy to realize that the scrambling noise from above had stopped. Instead there was a low grunting of pain, and then a sucking sound.

"What in the world?" the woman said, puzzled.

"Wait!" Jamieson whispered tensely.

They waited what must have been five minutes, then ten—half an hour. The sucking sound above was weaker. An overtone of wheezing accompanied it, and the grunts had stopped. Once there was a low, hoarse moan of agony.

"Help me up," Jamieson whispered. "I want to see how close it is to death."

"Listen," she snapped, "either you're mad or I'm going to be. For heaven's sake, what's it doing?"

"It smelled the blood on the knife," Jamieson replied, "and began to lick it. The licking cut its tongue into ribbons, which whipped it into a frenzy, because with every lick more of its own blood would flow into its mouth. You say it loves blood. For the last half hour it's been gorging itself on its own blood. Primitive stuff, common to many planets."

"I guess," Barbara Whitman said in a queer voice after a long moment, "there's nothing now to prevent us getting back to the Five Cities."

Jamieson stared with narrowed eyes at her vague shape in the darkness. "Nothing except—you!"

They climbed in silence to where the gryb lay dead. Jamieson was aware of Barbara watching him as he gingerly removed the knife from where it was wedged into the rock. Then, abruptly, harshly, she said, "Give me that!"

Jamieson hesitated, then handed the knife over. Outside, the morning greeted them, bleak yet somehow more inviting. The Sun was well above the horizon, and something else was in the sky, too: a huge red ball of pale fire, sinking now toward the western horizon. It was Carson's Planet.

The sky, the world of this moon, was lighter, brighter; even the rocks didn't look so dead or so black. A strong wind was blowing, and it added to the sense of life.

The morning seemed cheerful after the black night, as if hope were once again possible.

It's a false hope, thought Jamieson. The Lord save me from the stubborn duty sense of an honest woman. She's going to attack.

Yet, the attack, when it came, surpassed his expectations. He caught the movement, the flash of the knife, out of the corner of his eye and whipped aside. Her strength astonished him. The knife caught the resisting fabric of the arm of his electrically heated suit, scraped a foot-long scar on that obstinate, half-metallic substance, and then Jamieson was dancing away along a ledge of firm rock.

"You silly fool," he gasped. "You don't know what you're doing."

"You bet I know!" she said, panting. "I've got to kill you, and I'm going to in spite of your silver tongue. You're the devil himself for talking, but now you die."

She came forward, knife poised, and Jamieson let her come. There was a way of disarming a person attacking with a knife, providing the method was unknown to the attacker. She came at him silently; her free hand grabbed at Jamieson, and that was all he needed. Just a damned amateur who didn't know knife fighters didn't try for holds. Jamieson snatched at that striking hand, caught it with grim strength and jerked the woman past him with every ounce of his power. As she hurtled by him, propelled by her own momentum as well as by that arm-wrenching pull, Jamieson twisted along with her. At the last instant he braced himself for the shock and sent her strong young body spinning along like a top.

Frantically, the woman fought for balance. But there was no mercy in that rough ground. Jamieson made a strong leap and caught her as she started to fall over a section of upjutting rock. Caught her, held her, took the knife from her numbed fingers.

She looked up at him, and her eyes were suddenly wet with tears. Jamieson saw, relieved, that the hard surface was gone from her and that she was a woman again and not an agent of destruction. On faraway Earth, he had his own intensely feminine wife, and so from profound personal experience, he knew that she had given in and that from now on the danger was from the unfriendly planet and not from his companion.

All that morning Jamieson scanned the skies. She evidently expected no help, but he did. In the "west" Carson's Planet was engulfed by the blue, dark horizon of its moon, an age-old cycle repeating. The strong wind died, and there was quiet upon that wild, fantastic land.

About noon he saw what he had been looking for during all the morning hours—a moving dot in the sky. It came nearer and took the outline of a small aircraft.

It circled down and he saw with relief—but actually as he had anticipated—that it was from his own battleship. A hatch opened. An officer glanced down. "We looked for you all through the night, sir. But evidently you didn't think to carry any equipment we could detect."

"We had an unfortunate accident," said Jamieson quietly.

"You told us you were going to the uranium mines—which is in the opposite direction."

"All is well now, thank you," said Jamieson noncommittally.

A few moments later they were flying toward the safety and comforts of civilization.

Once aboard the great ship, Jamieson considered seriously what, if any, counteraction he should take, as a retaliation for the murder attempt that had been made against him. Two points were important. These people were too angry to understand mercy. They would misinterpret it as fear. And they were too prejudiced to accept punishment as justified.

His final decision was to do nothing. Make no complaint. File no charge. Regard it as another purely personal experience. He felt a sharp sadness as he came to that thought. It was a little hard for the rational men of the Earth Administration to realize that periodically the enemy was not the Rulls but other men. It was a weakness in men, for which there could never be an adequate reckoning. For entire groups of people, or for individuals, to sink below the necessary standards of courage and good sense—perhaps someday an adequate punishment would be devised in some superhuman court of justice. On that distant day, the accused would stand before the bar, and the charge would be: self-pity, excessive grief, inability to feel shame or guilt, failure to live up to human potentiality.

Barbara Whitman, in her own confused fashion, had realized something of that truth. And so, she had stayed to take the risks with him. But it was a mixed-up solution for a problem that could exist only in a world of fallen people.

Sometimes, as now, awareness would come to Jamieson of how vast was the number of human weaklings in a universe menaced by the remorseless Rull enemy.

En route to Earth, Jamieson sent a message ahead, inquiring if Commander McLennan had successfully landed with the captured mother ezwal and her cub.

The first reply was brief: "Slow ship. Not yet."

The second answer came two weeks later, only a day before the super-fast ship which carried Jamieson was due to reach Earth. Its import was electrifying. "News announcement received a few hours ago that the Mc-

Lennan ship was about to crash out of control in the Canadian north. Both ezwals expected to die in the crash. No further information about personnel of ship."

"Oh, my God!" said Jamieson aloud, in anguish. The message slipped out of his hands and floated to the floor of his suite.

VIII

THE GRIM FACE of Commander McLennan turned toward the two officers. "Absolutely out of control!" he said. "The ship will strike Earth in fifteen minutes somewhere in the Gulf of Alaska, perhaps as far west as the Peninsula."

He straightened, squaring his shoulders. "There's no help for it," he went on more calmly. "We checked the ship for damage as well as humanly possible in space, and none showed." His voice became crisp. "Carling, get the men started into the lifeboats, then make contact with the Aleutian Military Base. Tell them we've got two ezwals aboard, which may live through the crash. It won't quite be a free fall; residual antigravity will prevent that, even though the main power is dead. It means they must track this ship with every radar unit they've got, so they can pinpoint the spot where it hits and let us know quickly. If those monsters should get loose on the mainland, there's no telling how many people they'd kill. Got that?"

"Yes, sir!" Carling started away on the double.

"Just a minute!" McLennan called after him. "Get

this across—it's important—the ezwals are not to be harmed unless they do get loose. Bringing them here is a top-priority mission, and they are wanted by the government alive if possible. No one is to enter the wreck until I get there. That's all. Brenson!"

The white-faced younger officer stiffened to attention. "Yes, sir!"

"Take a couple of men below and see that every companion hatch above the main hold is closed and secured. That might hold those beasts a while if the cage breaks open. If they survive the crash at all, they ought to be plenty groggy, at least. Now get going, and be at the lifeboats in five minutes—no longer!"

Brenson blanched whiter still. "Yes, sir!" he said again, and was gone.

For McLennon there were vital things to do, valuable papers to retrieve. And then the time was up. As he approached the center lifeboat station, the whistling of air along the outer hull became audible. Carling saluted him nervously.

"All the men are aboard the lifeboats, sir—except Brenson."

"Damn Brenson! What's he doing down there? What about the men with him?"

"Apparently he went alone, sir. All the men are here."

"Alone? What the devil— Send somebody after him! No, never mind—I'll go myself."

"Excuse me, sir!" Carling's face was anguished. "There's no time! If we don't put off in the next two minutes, the slip stream may wreck us! Besides, there's something about Brenson you didn't know, sir. He was the wrong man to send below, I'm afraid."

McLennan stared. "Why? What about Brenson?"

"His older brother," said Carling, "was in the Colonial Guard, stationed on Carson's Planet, and was torn to bits by ezwals."

From above the young ezwal there sounded the terrible snarl of his mother; and then her thought, as hard and sharp as crystal: "Under me for your life! The two-legged one comes to kill!"

Like a streak, he leaped from his end of the cage, five hundred pounds of dark-blue monstrosity. Razor-clawed prehensile paws rattled metallically on the steel floor, and then he was into blackness under her vast form, pressing into the cave of yielding flesh that she made for him. He clamped himself to her flexible, incredibly tough skin with his hands, so that, no matter what the violence of her movements, he would be there safe and sound, snugly deep in the folds between her great belly muscles.

Her thought came again. "Remember all the things I've told you. The hope of our race is that men continue to think of us as beasts. If they suspect our intelligence, we are lost. And someone does suspect it. If that knowledge lives, our people die!"

Faster came her thought. "Remember, your worst weaknesses are those of youth. You love life too much. You must accept death if the opportunity comes to serve your race by so doing."

Her brain slowed; she grew calm. He watched with her then, clinging to her mind with his mind as tightly as his body clung to her body. He saw the thick steel bars of the cage; and, half hidden by their four-inch width, the figure of a man. He saw the *thoughts* of the man!

"You damned monsters! You'll never have a chance to murder another human being!" The man's hand moved. There was a metallic glint as he thrust a weapon between the bars. It spouted white fire. For a moment the mental contact with his mother blackened. It was his own ears that heard the gasping roar, his own flat nostrils that smelled the odor of burning flesh. And there was no mistaking the physical reality of her wild charge straight at the merciless flame gun projecting between the bars.

The fire clicked off. The blackness vanished from his mother's mind. The young ezwal saw that the weapon and the man had retreated from the reaching threat of those mighty claws.

"Damn you!" the man flared. "Well, take it from here then!"

There must have been blinding pain, but none of it came through into his brain. His mother's thoughts remained at a mind-shaking pitch of malignance, and not for an instant did she remain still. She ducked this way and that. She ran with twisting, darting, rolling, sliding movements as she fought for life in the narrow confines of the cage. But always, in spite of her desperation, a part of her mind remained untouched, unhurried. The tearing fire followed her, missing her, then hitting her squarely, hitting her so often that finally she could no longer hold back the knowledge that her end was near. And with that thought came another, his first awareness that she had a purpose in keeping the weapon beyond the bars, and forcing it to follow the swift, darting frenzy of her movements. In the very act of pursuing her, the beam of the flame gun had seared with fusing effect across the thick steel bars.

Now, in between the hissing bursts from the flame gun, a new strange sound could be heard, like an all-pervading, continuous sigh. It seemed to come from outside the hold, and it grew gradually louder, rising in pitch.

"God!" came the man's thoughts. "Won't this stinking beast ever die? I've got to get out of here—we've hit the air! And where is that damned young one? It must be—" The thought broke off in startlement as sixty-five hundred pounds of steel-thewed body smashed with pile-driver momentum at the weakened bars of the cage.

The cub strained with his own taut muscles against the contraction of that rocklike wall of muscle surrounding him—and lived. He heard and felt the metal bars bend and break, where the flame had lessened their tensile strength.

There was a gasping scream, and an image of the man standing there, with no bars intervening, his face going slack with mindless fright. The gun dropped from his limp hand, and as it clattered on the floor, he turned and ran, loose-kneed, toward the nearest companion-way. He half fell against the ladder and started up with difficulty, his limbs shaking almost uncontrollably.

Then the young ezwal felt the surge of his mother's body as it pressed free of its last restraint. In two great bounds, she covered the distance to the companionway ladder, so that the image of the man on it seemed to come at them with a rush. There was another scream, this one cut short by the single stroke of a slashing paw; then silence. And the scene faded into darkness.

Darkness! As the huge, enveloping form slumped and settled over him, the meaning of that darkness came to him, and a sense of loss that was almost unbearable. To the young ezwal, the death of his mother was doubly overwhelming; not only the physical assurance of that immensely capable body but the secure vantage point of that proud and forceful mind would be no more. These things he had taken for granted, and now, for the first time, he began to realize how great had been his dependence on them, especially during captivity. He was utterly, terrifyingly alone, and life had become intolerable. He wanted to die.

And yet, as he huddled in apathy, half suffocated by his mother's inert bulk, he became dully aware of two things. The first was a slightly dizzying sensation of lightness and a lessening of the oppressive weight upon him. The second was the sighing sound he had heard earlier, now increased to the proportions of a vast, low whistle. The ship was falling—and falling more freely with each passing moment!

Deep-seated instinct, touched by that sudden realization, prompted him to struggle free of the ponderous mass above him. The whistling sound was very loud now and more piercing. And the sensation of falling was becoming excruciating, as if the deck under him were about to be snatched away altogether at any moment. That deck was metal-hard and cold; he longed for the sanctuary of his mother's belly.

Instead, he leaped for her broad back, feeling the need for contact as much as for cushioning. But he jumped too high, having failed to allow for his reduced weight, and rolled off awkwardly on the far side. The outside air was shrieking against the hull now. He was clambering giddily from his dead mother's great flank out onto the expanse of her back, when sight and sound and all other sensation ended in the world-shattering crash.

IX

His FIRST RETURNING awareness was of pain. Every bone in his body obtruded its soreness into his reluctant brain; every muscle told of unmerciful strain and bruising. He yearned to retreat into unconsciousness, but there was something else that would not let him. Thoughts! A confusion of strange thoughts from the minds of many men. *Danger!*

Arousing, he found himself lying on the cold metal deck. Apparently he had slid or rolled from his mother's back, after her resilient flesh had absorbed enough of the fearful shock to save his life. Above him, the ship had split asunder, showing a dusky sky through the fissure, and along the visible side were half a dozen other gaping holes. Through them, a cold wind was blowing, and beyond them, the ground showed strangely white. Against that whiteness, dark figures moved about. As he looked, a beam of light lanced out from one of the openings and swung across the deck, passing close to him and fixing on his mother's great body. In a spasm of movement, avoiding the splash of light, he scuttled under her, pressed upward into the folds of her belly and clung there, quiveringly still.

Shouted words rang hollowly in the chamber, bounced at crazy angles from the twisted bulkheads and became hopelessly garbled. Not that they could mean anything to the ezwal. But the thought behind them was clear, and the man's mind which formed it held vast relief.

"Everything's all right, Commander! It's dead!"

There was an odd, shuffling sound, then the stamping of several pairs of feet on metal.

"What do you mean, *it's* dead?" a different, very assertive mind gave answer. "You mean the big one's dead, don't you? Here, give me that light."

"You don't suppose the little one could have—"

"Can't take anything for granted. And it isn't so little. Five hundred pounds, likely, and I'd sooner meet a full-grown Bengal tiger." Several beams of light now moved methodically about the chamber. "I only hope it hasn't got out of here already. There are a dozen places . . . Carling! Get twenty men around to the other side on the double and set up your floodlight in that biggest break. Don't forget to check the snow for tracks before you mess it up! What's the matter, Daniels?"

A wave of horror and revulsion was emanating from the man's mind. "It's—it's Brenson, sir—or what's left of him. By the ladder there."

Immediately the man's emotion was shared by the others in varying degree. It was followed by a mental stiffening and a dawning, bitter fury among them that caused the young ezwal to cringe in his hiding place.

"Damn shame!" came an explosive thought. "Fool thing to do, of course, but . . . Say! From the looks of that beast, it wasn't just the crash that did her in. The hide's half scorched off her! And look at the bars of that cage." There followed a fairly accurate conjecture as to what had happened, then: "Of course, if the young one was trapped under her," Commander McLennan finished, "it would have been crushed to a pulp. On the other hand . . . Parker!"

"Yes, sir!" Curiously, that answering thought did not come direct but was perceptible to the ezwal only as it registered in the commander's mind. Its sender, therefore, must be at some distance and communicating mechanically. The ezwal was aware that such things were possible.

"Bring your lifeboat right over the main crack in this hull. Drop a loop of cable over the middle leg of that beast and roll her over. Carling, did you see any tracks around the ship?"

"No, sir."

"Then there's a good chance it's still under its mother, dead or alive. Place your men to cover every opening on that side. Turn your floodlight over there where ours makes a shadow. Everybody on the alert now! If it comes out, shoot fast and shoot to kill!"

The ezwal let himself sink slowly in his cave of flesh. His nose caught a draft of air and twitched at the scent of cooked flesh from his mother's body. The memory it brought of fire and agony sent a sick thrill along his nerves.

He forced the fear aside and considered his chances. In their minds there had been pictures of brush and trees. That meant hiding places. But there was also a sense of white brightness, and somehow it connected with a cold, clinging wetness that obstructed the feet and would slow him down if by some miracle he got that far. But it was almost dark out there; that would help.

Then as he cautiously pressed aside a fold of flesh just far enough to reveal some of the scene beyond, his hopes faded, and the terrain outside the ship seemed very remote indeed. Glaring white light bathed the interior of the hold and tensely waiting men stood at the openings with drawn guns. The place was a deadly trap, as inescapable as fifty armed and determined men could make it. The young ezwal shrank back slowly lest his three-in-line eyes betray him by their reflected glitter. His mother had taught him that precaution as a part of stalking prey in the vast forests of his home world, now unthinkably far away.

Suddenly the walls of flesh encasing him moved and began to lift away! There was an electrifying moment as he imagined that his mother was stirring back to life; then panic gripped him as he realized the truth. They were turning her over! He froze, nearly blinded by the mounting flood of light. But the next instant it diminished, and simultaneously the wind was forced out of him by the descending mass. Something had slipped, apparently, and as the ezwal lay gasping for breath, the impatient directions of McLennan reached his mind.

"Parker! Move your lifeboat farther forward and bring the loop up closer to the body. . . . That's better. All right, try it again."

Once more the haven of his mother's body began to lift from him—and kept on lifting. The young ezwal cowered, drawing air painfully into his labored lungs. At any moment now the men would distinguish his body from the larger one. Then would come hideous pain—the same fire that had burned away his mother's life but multiplied many times over.

He stiffened at the thought of his mother's death, and he recalled what she had told him about fighting fear. She, too, had known certain doom, but she had burst through steel bars to get at her executioner and kill him with her last strength. These men were many—hopelessly many—but there were no bars in the way. If he moved fast enough . . .

All fear was now gone, dispersed by the intensity of his terrible purpose. In another instant, the lifting mass above him would leave the way clear. He drew a deep breath and set his rear feet carefully against the most solid flesh he could feel behind him.

Now! Like a releasing spring, the ezwal launched himself straight at the nearest group of men, thirty yards away. As he did so, a wave of startlement and alarm from the minds of many human beings burst in upon him with an almost physical force. It was instantly followed by a unanimous and deadly intent: *Kill it! Kill it!* The weapons held by the three men directly before him were only a few of dozens being aimed at him in that moment, with fingers tightening on their triggers.

Still half blinded by the glare, he did not see an open seam between two warped deck plates until one of his feet slipped into it and wedged itself. By a fantastically quick reflexive action he was able to fling his entire body to one side in time to jerk his foot free without snapping the bones. But as a result he rolled completely over and slid helplessly into a ten-foot hole where a large section of the deck had collapsed.

The unplanned maneuver saved his life—for the moment. As he hit bottom, the air above him crackled with the convergent fires of a dozen blasters.

There was a dark, jagged opening in one side of the hole, large enough for him to squeeze through. It probably led to a lower level which might or might not give access to the outside. He decided against it. That level must have been crushed worse than this one and could easily be a fatal trap.

The nearest men would reach the edge of the hole any second. Gauging as nearly as he could the direction from which they would be approaching, he set himself and leaped. He cleared the torn, sharp rim of the hole with a little to spare and landed within reach of the first oncoming man. He reached. Blood spattered as the man went down like a tenpin, his gun discharging harmlessly into the air.

Without hesitation, the ezwal plunged at the two men beyond him. They had held their fire briefly because of the first man, and now it was too late. The ezwal smashed into one with bonebreaking force and slashed the other's chest and stomach to tatters in passing. Resisting an impulse to pause and crunch their bodies with his teeth, the ezwal made for the nearest opening in the hull, only twenty feet away. The next moment he was through it with a bound and veering sharply to one side. Almost as he did so, a roaring mass of flame rolled through the opening and lighted up the snow-covered scene starkly.

Snow! His feeling of fierce triumph diminished sharply as the strange white stuff, cold and soft, slowed his limbs to half their potential fleetness.

And now a bright beam of light stabbed out of the ship behind him, swung dazzlingly across the snow and threw his own elongated shadow out before him. It also illumined a great boulder just ahead. The ezwal dodged into the blackness beyond it. Behind him the boulder was struck by savage flame. There was an earsplitting hiss, and the boulder fell apart into rubble. The flame surged on, reaching with incandescent violence above him as he dived into a shallow arroyo. But here the snow had drifted, soft and deep, and he floundered with exasperating slowness. After a little way, he risked taking to the rocky ridge which bounded the arroyo, running along just below the top on the side farthest from the ship.

Twice he dipped lower as searching beams of light raked the ridge but failed to find him. Then, glancing back, he caught sight of something that caused his rising hopes to sink to a new low. The lifeboat was sweeping straight toward him along the ridge at a rate he could not equal. From its underside, half a dozen search beams fanned out to the ground, making a swath of light much too wide to evade. The only shelter which could hide him was a clump of trees too far ahead to reach in time. The ship would be over him in seconds.

There was a group of boulders close by, half buried in snow, the nearest of them twenty feet away. Gathering himself, he leaped for it, so as to leave no tracks in the softer snow intervening. Landing on top of it, he instantly poised and leaped again in a high arc, coming straight down in the middle of the group of rocks with his legs tucked under him. He thrust his head into the snow, arched his supple back into an unnatural hump and held himself rigid.

He could not see the lights as the ship passed over him, but the thoughts of the watchers in it gave no sign of detection. The pilot was evidently in communication with the commander back at the wreck, and an earlier situation was being reversed. This time it was the pilot's thoughts which came to the ezwal directly.

"I don't see how it could have got much farther than this, sir, but there's no sign of it."

"Are you sure it didn't turn off the ridge anywhere?"

"Yes, sir. The snow is deep on both sides. It couldn't have got off without making tracks. And there's no place to hide. Wait a minute. There's a clump of trees and brush just ahead—the only one around here. I'm not sure our lights can penetrate it sufficiently to—"

"Better land and search it. For God's sake be careful! We've had enough casualties already."

The ezwal relaxed his uncomfortable position but did not leave his hollow in the snow. It was melting with his body heat and enlarging to overly revealing proportions around him. And all six extremities, immersed in as many pools of freezing water, were growing numb. On the tropical world of his origin, there was water in abundance, but in temperature it ranged from tepid to hot. The young animal longed for that world with his whole being.

Abruptly he alerted himself. The men were returning to their lifeboat.

"It's not there, sir. We've had a look at every sqaure foot of it."

There was a pause; then: "All right, Parker. Circle the area a couple of more times, higher up, and see if there is any place it could be hiding. In the meantime, call the other lifeboat. It should be well on its way to the base by now. Tell them as soon as they get the wounded men to the hospital to pick up those hunting dogs and bring them back here. The superintendent says he can get ten. With them, we can follow that young monster's trail, tracks or no tracks. And I'll guarantee they can wear all six legs off it in the long haul!"

The ezwal watched tensely as the lifeboat lifted from

the ground, but it moved off to the left, gaining altitude. As soon as it had withdrawn a safe distance, he leaped back to the ridge, raced along it to within jumping distance of the clump of trees, and took cover under its drooping boughs. Here he should be safe until the circling lifeboat left the vicinity.

Five minutes later he halted on the rock lip of a wide valley that curved away dimly into the distance. Here were many more trees and wilder, more broken terrain, snow-covered and softly gleaming in the starry, moonless night. Off to his left, the sky was faintly aglow with an oddly pulsating light. It might mean anything, in this strange world, but it could be evidence of human habitation. That direction was to be avoided.

He leaped from the ledge and started down into the valley at a steady, swift gait. Here the snow was packed harder, and he found he could proceed without making deep tracks, especially if he skirted the drifts. That would make it impossible for the human beings to follow him by air, or at least they would be limited to the speed of the dogs. The picture of the latter had not been clear, but he had gathered that dogs were smaller than human beings and less intelligent, but with as keen a sense of smell as his own.

X

GRAY DAYLIGHT was spreading slowly over the snowy, forested hills before the young ezwal stopped to rest. For this purpose, he chose a cranny under an overhanging ledge, out of the snow and sheltered from the bitter wind. During the long hours of the night, he had fought the unaccustomed cold by the continuous activity of running, and his magnificent body machine had circulated adequate heat to his extremities. But now he huddled with his limbs against his body, and it was not until he had warmed the surface of the surrounding wall of rock that he became comfortable enough to doze.

Some indefinite time later, a timid thought touched his mind, partly fear, partly curiosity, mostly stupidity. For a moment, in that half-awakened state, it seemed to be his own awareness.

It took an instant to reject those characteristics; they so very definitely did not apply to him. Startled when he realized that it was an alien mental intrusion, the ezwal opened his eyes.

A deer nibbled at a few sparse tufts of brown grass it had uncovered on a slope a short distance away. It kept rolling its eyes, half turning its head; and its thought pattern remained the same dull composite of hunger urge and alertness to danger.

Food? With hungry eyes, the ezwal studied the creature and evaluated his chance of making a kill. There was much snow between, of varying depth and solidity; most of the impetus for the attack would have to come from his initial spring. Carefully the ezwal drew his legs under him, dug first one clawed foot, then another into the hard ground, and tensed himself for the charge.

The flesh was edible; that was all. He swallowed hastily, to get the taste of it out of his mouth. Several times he plunged his mouth into a bank of snow and let the chill wetness of it cleanse the blood taste and the blood feel out of him. He was distastefully rinsing his mouth in this fashion, once again, when a sound floated on the still air.

Animal yelping!

The sound was far away, but a faint overtone of thought came with it: human thought, human purpose. With a thrill of concern, the ezwal guessed that these were the bloodhounds, and this was the hunt—for him.

He leaped to a ridge for a better view. He stretched upward on his rear legs and angled his neck. From that height he could see his footprints in the distance of the valley he had spanned the evening before. The route he had followed stood out in the snow; it was unmistakable—too straight, too easy to follow. It shook his confidence; and he was about to leap down, and away, when a shadow flitted across the snow.

The ezwal froze. A moment later an air machine passed by less than a quarter of a mile to his right and settled down in the valley a mile away, near his back trail. An opening appeared in its side. From the opening sprang five dogs. Swiftly they plunged in all directions; and their eagerness was plainly audible in the excited yelps they gave. Even as the ezwal watched, one of them found his trail and bayed. A minute later the five beasts were heading toward him across the snow.

The ezwal had the impulse to run directly away from that menace. Instead, after one mental flip of fear, he began to follow the rocky ridge up into the higher mountains, away from the rising sun. The going was not easy. Where it was not covered with snow, the ground was rough; and, as he stumbled along—now running, now slowed to a walk, now cautiously leaping a dangerous crevice—he had the unhappy feeling that the bloodhounds were racing straight at him. Or that at any moment their human masters would soar overhead and blast him from this precarious height. In his mind's eye, he visualized a second airship picking up other dogs farther back on the trail and bringing them forward to a new, closer point on his trail.

Abruptly he turned from the ridge and swiftly plunged down the steep slope. Again changing his direction, he cut across a narrow valley toward a farther ridge, automatically avoiding the easiest course, instinctively hiding his footprints wherever possible. He did not, however, make an obsession of concealment. There were times, then, when the baying of the dogs faded into vast distance or was lost in the reach of snow-filled valleys. But always the sound returned. And each time he felt spurred to drive his tiring body to new effort. When at last the reddish sun began to sink between two distant, craggy peaks and the long shadows grew darker, the ezwal guessed wearily that for this day he was now safe.

He had been planning for the moment. In great leaps, and with all his reserve strength, he bounded across a range of hills, at right angles to the course he had been pursuing—and, at a distance of several hundred yards, headed back the way he had been coming all these hours.

Presently, from the comparative safety of a brush-covered elevation, he looked down into a valley, where two ships rested on the ground near each other. Tiny figures of men moved about in the snow, and to one side in the shelter of a bluff the dogs were being fed. The hunters seemed to be camping for the night.

The ezwal did not wait to make sure. As the shadows of approaching night lengthened over that bleak land, he headed down the mountainside. He had to circle wide; the twilight wind was erratic. And so, seeking a windward approach, he came to the top of the bluff.

With glowing eyes, he stared down from his vantage point at ten dogs. They were chained in a bunch, some already asleep in the snow. A horrible, alien smell drifted up from them, and he guessed that as a pack they were dangerous. But if he could kill these dogs, other beasts like them would have to be flown in. And he might have time to lose himself in these miles of forest and mountain.

He would have to be murderously quick, though. The men could tumble out of those ships in seconds and come at him with their irresistible guns.

The thought sent him hurtling down the slope, faster than the snowslide he dislodged.

The first dog saw him. He caught the startled thought as it lunged to its feet, heard its sharp warning yelp and felt the blackness snap into its brain as he dealt it one crushing blow. He whirled; and his jaws swung precisely into the path of the dog that was charging at his neck. Teeth that could dent metal clicked in one ferocious, stabbing bite. Blood gushed into his mouth, stingingly, bitterly unpleasant to his taste. He spat it out with a thin snarl as eight shrieking dogs leaped at him. He met the first with a claw-armored forehand upraised.

The wolfish jaws slashed at the blue-dark, descending arm, ravenous to tear it to bits. But in his swift way, the ezwal avoided the reaching teeth and caught at the neck. And then, claws like steel clamps gripped deep into the shoulders; and the dog was flung like a shot from a gun to the end of its chain. The chain snapped from the force of the blow, and the dog slid along in the snow and lay still. Its neck was broken. The ezwal reared around for a plunge at the others—and stopped. The dogs were surging away from him, fear thoughts in their minds. They were beaten—utterly cowed.

He paused there making certain. Men were shouting, lights flashing. But still he explored the thoughts and feelings of the dogs. Finally, there was no doubt. They were terrified of him. This particular group of dogs had ceased to be dangerous to him. They could not, he felt sure, be whipped into following him now.

The ezwal turned to run. A searchlight caught him full in the face, startling him into panicky flight. Whoever was manipulating the light lacked skill, for it lost him almost immediately. When he was already safe beyond another slope, someone belatedly began to fire a flame rifle at the shadows behind him. The explosions lighted the sky.

He slept that night contentedly. At dawn he was on his way. It was midafternoon before he heard the baying of the dogs again. The sound shocked him, for he had tended to fool himself a little, to hope in spite of reason, that by pushing himself to the uttermost limit, he would somehow gain safety in this wasteland.

He raced on, a great tiredness in him; not only was he physically exhausted but his will to live was dimmed. For he could not imagine that he would be able successfully to attack this new pack of dogs. However, as darkness settled, he tried. As before, he retraced his steps, cunningly, warily, with every perception keyed to danger. His telepathic mind detected the expected ambush from a safe distance.

He retreated, baffled and anxious, into the darkness. On and on he padded over the snowy ground. The night grew blacker as clouds slowly blotted out the stars; only the dim whiteness of the snow enabled him to see clearly enough to avoid hazards.

It grew colder. Soft flakes began to fall, ever more slantingly as a wind from the north blew lightly at first, then with driving violence.

All through that long night he fought the blizzard and the cold. For in it he divined the safety he had been seeking. Once more his goal was to put distance between himself and his pursuers, with the knowledge that this time his trail was covered by miles of drifting snow.

The first dull light of dawn found the storm abating. But its ragged edges continued gustily. It was a cold, miserable, hungry young ezwal that espied a cavernous opening in a steep slope and wearily started to enter. In the shadows of the entrance, he stopped. A shape was rearing up from the interior, a massive dark creature.

The surprise was mutual and intense. The exhausted ezwal took in the dank odor of animal warmth, the musty smell of droppings and the sudden surge of thought feelings that radiated toward him—and he guessed that he had caught the monster sound asleep.

Another bear daring to intrude . . . outrage . . . a desperate need to throw off the dullness of long sleep —those were the idea forms from the Kodiak bear. Seeing only a large shape, and that but dimly, the beast came up out of apathy into berserk rage within moments, snarled hideously and charged.

The impact sent the ezwal sliding backward in the snow, but not far. His taloned paws gripped the frozen surface, and in his own solid fashion, he held his ground and bit without mercy into the colossal shoulder that pressed forward against him.

The bear reacted with a roar and a grasping, hugging action that pulled the lighter ezwal almost off his rear legs into an embrace that shocked the breath from his lungs. For a moment, then, the ezwal struggled weakly to break away, feeling himself too weary to fight a death battle with so powerful a beast.

The attempt was a serious mistake. He had already caught from the other its first awareness of the alien thing that it was fighting. A tinge of fear, a foolish amazement, a dumb desire to withdraw and consider the situation. But as the ezwal tried to pull away, the change in the mighty Kodiak was swift. It tightened its grip. With its long jaws, it slashed at the ezwal's body, laying open a painful gash.

The beast growled in awful triumph; and now its thought flow was all rage and savagery and lust to kill. It freed one massive paw and swung with surprising speed.

It was a staggeringly hard blow. The ezwal felt the shock of it in a momentary blackout. For an instant the pain galvanized him out of his weariness and for a brief period he was himself. He bit at the retreating paw, and his movement was so rapid that his teeth closed on it. A twitch of his head severed tendons and crushed bones. Simultaneously, he brought his middle legs into play and raked the bear's belly with long talons, tearing the hide, ripping the stomach wall, gouging deep into the body cavity of the half-ton beast in one cycle of action.

The counterattack was so violent it should have ended the struggle. But the bear was too far gone in rage to recognize the hideous damage it had suffered. Had the ezwal been less weary, he could have escaped at that moment. As it was, the bear uttered a scream and, in the blindness of its pain, knew only enough to repeat its madness. Once more it clutched its smaller antagonist in a desperate embrace. But those great arms had never before held such an engine of destruction.

The ezwal could not react swiftly. But speed was not needed. Tiredly, he brought his middle legs into position. Tiredly, he ripped down. This time, whole masses of the bear's vitals were actually torn from its body.

No bestial fury could sustain it further against such devastation. In a vast, dumb surprise, the bear fell in the snow. Still clutching the ezwal, it gasped bloody foam—and died.

The ezwal lay exhausted in that dead embrace, until finally the bear jerked in an insensate muscular convulsion, and the ponderous forelegs relaxed. The ezwal extricated himself painfully and staggered into the cave.

The unpleasant bear smell inside did not deter him. He licked his wounds clean and curled himself into a warm ball. And slept.

XI

HE AWAKENED ONCE with the mental impression that there were animals nearby. The impression was sharp enough to include awareness of size. And, though there were many, the size feeling he got was of animals much smaller than the bear.

There was an over-all mental flow of utter bestiality— which reassured him. No danger from human beings so long as such creatures felt safe. He gathered from sounds and mind pictures that they were eating the bear. The ezwal slept again. When he awakened, it was still daylight, and the wolves were mostly gone. The ezwal had a flash of scenes of bones and fur scattered over the snow and the impression that four beasts remained. Two of these were trying to crack a thigh bone. The telepathic picture he had was not clear on what one of the others was doing. But the remaining beast was in the act of sniffing at the entrance of the cave.

The ezwal glided to his feet, fully alert, energy surging into his muscles. At his first awkening he had been too weary to worry about being cornered. Now, strong again, he padded toward the entrance—reached it as the wolf cautiously nosed forward. At a distance of a few feet they looked at each other.

More savagery than had been in the dogs, or even the bear—that was the thought impact. And yet, after one long, toothy snarl, the wolf backed off, turned tail and slunk away. The ezwal read in its thoughts, not fear, but a healthy respect. He recognized in certain overtones, also, a hunger satiation. The wolf with a full stomach had no real interest in worrying a strange creature, larger and more powerful-looking than any three or four wolves.

The ezwal was nervous now. He felt a great urgency to hide all traces of the bear's death. It seemed to him that the scattered bones and tufts of fur and the blood-stained snow, as well as the very considerable animal tramping marks, would be clearly observable from the air.

He was acutely aware that he had slept through most of the day, too exhausted to be concerned. But the ability to be anxious was back in force. He went outside.

There were two wolves near, two more a hundred yards or so distant. The near ones looked at him from rage-filled eyes, but they retreated as he advanced, leaving the bones they had been chewing. Ignoring them, the ezwal buried everything he could find, smoothed over the snow as well as he could. And then backed step by step into the cave, covering his tracks as he went.

He slept all night, peacefully, in the heart of the hillside. The following day he slept fitfully, feeling the pangs of returning hunger. About mid-afternoon, snow began to fall. As the white drift from the sky thickened, the ezwal ventured from the cave. He had a definite goal. He recalled that he had crossed a frozen stream not far away and remembered other such streams, where he had sensed the presence of life forms under the ice. It was worth investigating.

He broke the ice at a point where the stream ran swiftly below and crouched beside it to wait. Rudimentary thoughts emanated from the water, now near, now far. Twice he saw glinting shapes in the swirling stream and merely observed their quick, jerky movements.

The third time he lowered his right foreleg into the icy water and held it there, and held it, and held it . . . until the fish was close.

Then he flicked his paw, in a single lightning thrust. Spray and fish came flying out onto the ice. He ate the tidbit with enjoyment. It had a pleasing flavor, unlike the deer.

It required an hour to catch and eat four more of the fish. The success left him still unsatisfied, but the edge was off his hunger. It was getting dark as he returned to the cave.

Thoughtfully he settled himself for the night. He was well aware that the overwhelming problems of the past few days were solved—and far better than his expectations. He now had sanctuary from his enemies, adequate shelter—even an unhoped-for source of palatable food. All of these things he had accomplished on his own, as the first real test of self-reliance in his young life, and he felt sure his mother would have been vastly proud of him, could she have known.

But in spite of all this, he was aware of a vague feeling of dissatisfaction. He had, after all, only secured his own escape; he had done little or nothing to avenge his mother's death.

How many human lives would it take to do that?

He decided that there were hardly enough human be-ings on this planet for the purpose. Certainly there were far too few in this remote part of it; and, on the realistic side, he could see very little chance of getting to the more densely populated areas.

Still, from the minds of his pursuers, he had gathered fleeting glimpses of villages and settlements hereabouts. Eventually it ought to be possible for him to reach one or more of them and achieve at least a partial account-ing of vengeance before he was killed.

But not yet. It would be foolish to imagine that the hunt was over. He would do well to expose himself as little as possible for the next several days and there-after to take advantage of snow flurries to work his way out of the hills.

On the fourth day after that, something happened which changed his plans. As he was moving along the stream bed looking for a likely place to fish, he stepped into a beaver trap with his rearmost left foot.

The snap of the metal jaws made him jump. The instant pain caused him to jerk away violently. It was that reaction which injured his foot severely, for his strength was so great that he ripped the flesh and dam-aged the tendons.

The ezwal crouched in agony and examined the in-strument that had caught him. In a few moments he had analyzed how it worked. He pressed down on the flat ends and lifted out his foot, which was now pulsing with pain. Soon afterward he started on downstream on five legs. He would have liked to go back to the cave and stay till his foot healed. But he dared not.

How soon they would discover the sprung trap and whether they would connect it with him were moot questions. But there could be little doubt that this was no longer safe territory.

Toward dawn he found himself a place to rest under

an overhanging rock. And he slept there most of the day. As the afternoon waned, he emerged cautiously onto the stream bed and, finding where the ice was thinnest over swift water, used a heavy rock to break through. Presently, he had caught some fish.

All that night, too, he moved along the stream bed. And the next.

On the third day he awoke from a deep sleep to the familiar sound of hissing jets. The ezwal watched tensely from his shelter as a small aircraft moved along a few dozen feet above the stream bed, heading in his direction.

As he drew back out of sight, a clear thought, seemingly directed straight at him, touched his mind.

"Leave this stream immediately. Your footsteps have been seen, and the search has begun. My name is Jamieson and I am trying to get authorization to save your life. But it may arrive too late. Leave this stream immediately. Your footprints have been seen. . . ."

The airship cruised on downstream, out of sight, and out of his thought-perception range. The young ezwal crouched where he was a moment longer, thinking tensely, "Was this a trap designed to get him out into the open while daylight still remained?"

He decided not. Here was one of the men who had guessed the ezwal secret. Actually, his friendship—while real in a limited sense—was more dangerous to the ezwal race than the death of his mother or himself.

The young ezwal felt a great reluctance to die without a struggle. Like a runner beginning a race, he darted from his concealment, heading upstream, the direction from which he had come. Early that morning he had gone by a deep indentation that made a jagged rocky valley stretching away from the stream in either direction; it was not far away.

He reached it, and his foot began to ache again. Ignoring the pain, he bounded along what seemed to be the more impassable of the two routes. The rocky pathless terrain led higher and higher, and presently he was on a crest several hundred feet above the stream.

Still there was no aircraft in sight, and no sign of the pursuers. Relieved, the ezwal headed for the higher pass that he could see in the distance ahead.

Night was falling as he ran over a land that seemed an endless wintry desolation. A gibbous moon came up behind him, and the sky to his right came alive with the strange lights which he had come to recognize as a peculiarity of the planet itself.

Interminably later, the first streaks of sunlight found him tired and with a foot that throbbed without letup. Much more disturbing, the brightening world ahead revealed a seacoast with a scattering of human habitations and, as far as the eye could see, a gray ocean.

The ezwal paused uncertainly and looked about. In a way, this was the sort of place he had been looking for; here were many human beings on which to begin wreaking his vengeance. But not while the hunt was still relatively close, and not while his lame foot hampered his every move.

He would have to skirt this settlement to the right or left, turn inland again and lie low until—

Suddenly, from over a nearby group of trees, a low-flying aircraft appeared and was above his head in an instant. The ezwal was off like a flash, but not before he recognized the same ship he had seen the day before at the creek. Now it followed him easily, matching his every twist and turn, and from it, the same clear mind which had addressed him the day before now projected a series of sharp, rapid thoughts.

"I will not harm you! If I wanted to, you would be dead. Stop running or you will be seen! You have already been seen by others hereabouts, and your presence reported. Knowing what direction you came from, I was able to find you first. But this entire area has been alerted, and the other ships are searching it. Stop running or you will be seen!"

The ezwal felt helpless—torn between this strong appeal to his sense of caution and a burning frustration at being unable to shake off his immediate pursuer. But less than a minute later the question was settled for him. He saw a scattered group of houses ahead, reversed his direction, and saw one of the dreaded lifeboats moving slowly along less than a mile off. He dived into a clump of bushes and cowered there, quivering.

Promptly, the small ship dropped like a stone and eased to a neat landing fifty feet away. The ezwal gave a start as a sliding after-hatch flew open, but no one emerged. Instead came urgent thoughts.

"Yesterday I tried to direct you toward open country, but now that you have come into this settled part, there is only one way I can save your life. You must get into the aft compartment and let me take you to where you will be safe. No, I cannot set you free again, but I believe I can guarantee that you will not be harmed. The other ship is coming closer! The men on it do not believe that you are an intelligent creature or anything but a menace to human lives, and there is no time to convince them of the truth. They will kill you unless you act quickly! Do you understand?"

The lifeboat was now only a few hundred yards away, hovering over a patch of underbrush much like the one the ezwal was hiding in. They were evidently searching it closely.

The ezwal waited tensely. His tracks, he was sure, were indistinguishable in the slushy, trampled snow, and there was a chance the lifeboat would turn elsewhere. But then, as he watched, it rose and drifted straight toward him.

"Quickly!" came the urgent plea from the smaller ship. "It will be much better if they do not see you enter."

Still the ezwal hesitated, bitterly reluctant to give up his hard-won freedom, even to save his own life. Then, at the last possible moment, it was not the consideration of his personal safety that decided him; it was the recollection of something his would-be protector had said: *"The men on it do not believe that you are an intelligent creature . . ."* It could mean the man in the waiting ship was the only one who did. And if that man could be killed, that knowledge might die with him.

XII

KEEPING HIS BODY low to the ground and taking advantage of intervening bushes, the ezwal glided rapidly toward the ship and leaped through the hatchway. The door clicked shut behind him, enclosing him in blackness, but not before he had seen that the inside of the compartment was featureless except for two small ventilator openings. As the deck rose abruptly under him, he settled wearily to his haunches and remained there.

Strangely, the realization that there would be no immediate opportunity to kill the possessor of the vital secret brought no particular feeling of chagrin but only a dull acceptance of the fact that matters must now take their course regardless of anything he might do.

And now, from somewhere outside the ship, came thoughts which registered simultaneously on the mind of the man sitting in the next compartment and also made sounds, faintly audible, through the metal bulkhead. "Dr. Jamieson! Always beating us to the spot, it seems. Haven't seen anything of that poor, misjudged little monster, have you?" This was the same forceful mind which had given orders at the wreck, many days before, and it now held an ill-concealed animosity.

There was a pause, then a carefully ironical reply. "I'm quite sure he has left the area, Commander McLennan."

"Indeed? Well, we'll soon know. There are six dogs on the trail, with the other lifeboat following them. Nice, fresh scent, too, judging from their speed. This time we won't stop till we catch up with it, wherever it is. Too bad you weren't able to persuade the commissioner that the beast was harmless enough to attempt capturing it alive—but maybe they'll let you have it stuffed."

While the commander spoke, his direct thoughts grew fainter, and the ezwal could feel Jamieson's small ship picking up horizontal speed. The next instant, Jamieson showed concerned awareness that the lifeboat was circling back rapidly.

"Jamieson!" It was Commander McLennan's voice and thought, both of which had furious overtones. "You will land your ship immediately, or we will be forced to blast you out of the air!"

The ezwal read dismay and bafflement in the mind of the man in the next compartment. There was also indecision, a mental debate whether to operate the controls in such a way as to bring the ship down to a landing or in another way which would send the ship dodging at full speed among the mountains and low-hanging clouds. But none of this uncertainty was apparent in Jamieson's indignant reply.

"What is the meaning of this, Commander?"

"Bluffing won't do you any good, Jamieson! One of the local residents saw the whole thing from his house on a hillside back there. Saw your ship maneuvering around, got his binoculars, and watched you land. Saw the beast enter your ship. What did you do—tempt it with a morsel of food from its own planet? I warn you, Jamieson, our guns are locked on your ship. If you have not started down by the count of three I shall give the order to fire! One . . . two . . ."

The ezwal felt the deck under him start to sink away. But just before that, he had been aware of a flashing series of thoughts in Jamieson's mind—a picturization of the ship being shot down, of Jamieson himself being killed by the crash, of the ezwal surviving long enough to be killed by the merciless weapons of those in the other ship. And along with the pictures, there was a sense of frustration and of keen regret at the failure of a vitally important plan.

It was very strange. This man's mind seemed quite different from that of the man who had slain the ezwal's mother. In this mind there was no will to destroy those in the other ship, even though they had threatened his life. Also, there was little if any personal fear.

And now there came a hurried stream of thoughts from the next compartment, aimed at him. "There is no time to explain to you at length, but you must understand one vitally important thing. You know, of course, why ezwals have chosen to conceal their intelligence: they fear a stiffening of opposition if human beings discover it. That would be quite true—if neither side had any more right to Carson's Planet than the other. As mere animals, which you ezwals pretend to be, you can have no such right under Interstellar Law. But as intelligent beings and original inhabitants you would have the clearest possible title.

"Ezwals can never drive human beings from Carson's Planet by brute force; but as one scientifically developed race to another, you can ask us to leave, as soon as you can defend your planet, and we shall be obliged to do so.

"I have staked my professional reputation—and my personal safety—on bringing you before the authorities of my government in the hope of proving to them that you and your kind are intelligent creatures and that we must stop killing and start bargaining with you. Naturally, I cannot do this without your full cooperation."

Even as the man finished speaking, a slight jar indicated the ship had touched ground. He had tested the walls of the compartment by pressing against them with all his strength, but there was no apparent weakness anywhere. The two groups of drilled holes which formed the ventilator openings showed the surrounding steel panels to be nearly as thick as the length of his claws.

Jamieson was speaking again, rather hastily. "The men in the other ship, as you probably know, are military men, assigned to track you down and capture you, dead or alive. When I arrived on Earth a few days ago and learned of this situation, I asked to be placed in charge, since Commander McLennan had been unsuccessful in locating you. But my request was refused because I emphasized the importance of taking you alive, and you were considered too great a menace. I am here against the wish of McLennan. He feels the military are better equipped to handle this kind of situation."

The ezwal was receiving Jamieson's account with only part of his mind; another part was increasingly aware of the pressure of thoughts from outside. They were mixed thoughts, some of them hostile—and some of that hostility seemed to be directed toward Jamieson. There seemed to be a feeling that the man had played the game unfairly. But here and there was a tinge of admiration for the way in which Jamieson had accomplished what they would have considered impossible.

The medley of thoughts had increased steadily in strength during the last few minutes, and now it remained constant. The other ship had evidently landed close by.

Jamieson finished urgently. "The situation is now out of my hands. But you can help us both by letting me know what McLennan has in mind—what his plans are— as soon as they become apparent to you. Or are you already aware of them?"

The ezwal sat back disdainfully on his haunches. He had not yet actually admitted to anything. And he would certainly not be trapped into an admission by such a shallow ruse, even though there was no evidence that the man had intended it that way.

XIII

AND NOW the pictures from Jamieson's mind showed that he had opened the control-room door and was stepping out to face several men whose guns were trained on him.

The voice of McLennan, who was still in the other ship, came from the loud-speaker. "Doctor, I'm too astonished right now at your illegal act to decide what I'll do about it. Step aside."

Jamieson made no reply but moved away from the ship as directed.

McLennan said gruffly, "All right, Carling, you may proceed."

One of the men, who was carrying a small metal cylinder, went to the control compartment just vacated by Jamieson and stepped inside. There followed a series of metallic sounds; then Jamieson spoke sharply. "I warn you, Commander, if you harm that ezwal as a helpless prisoner you will have a hard time justifying yourself."

"Have no fear, Dr. Jamieson—your playmate will not be harmed. I merely consider it necessary to inspect the compartment to see whether it is adequate to transport such a dangerous beast into civilization. The gas will merely render the animal unconscious for a period of a few hours."

"It won't affect this one," said Jamieson, "because he has had advance warning."

"Ah, yes," said the commander ironically. "Your pet theory. Well, we'll see if he's clever enough to stop breathing for several minutes. Carling, are you hooked up yet? If so, open the valve."

"Yes, sir."

The ezwal was taking his third deep breath as the hissing sound began, and he held it. He had no exact idea how long several minutes might be, so he lay there inertly, resolved to hold his breath into unconsciousness if necessary.

Meanwhile, outside the ship, Jamieson said, "I tell you, Commander, you will be making a dangerous mistake if you rely on the gas to immobilize that creature."

"You are asking us to believe," said McLennan, "that the beast knows we are gassing it merely because we have been talking about it—in short, that it understands our speech?"

"It reads minds."

The statement seemed to stop McLennan. The ezwal caught the change in the man's thought, the sudden partial acceptance of what Jamieson was saying.

McLennan spoke slowly. "Are you serious, sir?"

"Never been more serious in my life. Ezwals are perfect telepaths, the only telepaths in the universe that we know of who can both receive from and send to non-telepaths."

McLennan said speculatively, "It would be an ideal situation if we could have such a telepath aboard every ship."

"It would indeed," said Jamieson, "and that is only one of the many possibilities."

McLennan's hesitation ended. He was a man of a decisive turn of mind, and he said now, with finality, "That still leaves us the problem of making sure he remains a prisoner and does no more damage. Carling, give him another five minutes of that gas. Then open the door."

Five minutes, thirty . . . sixty minutes—it would have made no difference. Ezwals were amphibians, and an hour and a half would have been more like the time needed to make certain that an ezwal was properly anesthetized.

For the ezwal, the half acceptance by McLennan of Jamieson's theory crystallized the decision it had to make. It was now or never. Jamieson must die—in such a way that McLennan's momentary belief in the intelligence of ezwals would be shattered forever in a bestial display.

He moved, so that he could act instantly; then he let his body go limp. He became aware that Jamieson was stepping up to the machine, unnoticed. The scientist must have looked in because Jamieson spoke sharply. "Commander, I demand that you end the use of this gas. No one knows the effect of such a gas on an ezwal."

"It's what you used when you captured them."

"We were lucky."

McLennan said, "All right, Carling. Open that door. Stand back, everybody."

"What do you intend to do?" That was Jamieson.

"If he's unconscious we'll just hoist him over into the big machine here."

Jamieson seemed resigned. "Let me put the harness over him."

The ezwal had a mental picture of Jamison as he stepped toward the opening door of the compartment, and that changed his mind completely. He had intended to remain dormant for the time being and merely hope that some indefinite chance would bring Jamieson within his reach. Now, here was the man in an easy position for the kill. The ezwal gathered his legs under him and sprang across the widening path of light to the doorway.

The door opened all the way. The ezwal and the man stood face to face. Three-in-line steel-bright eyes were on a level with the steady, unwavering pair of brown ones.

From beyond, from the wintry outside, there was a nervous bustle, a tensing of several minds. The ezwal was aware, and then he put the awareness into the background of his thought.

An astonishing thing was happening. In spite of his desperate purpose, he was hesitating. Dimly, he understood why. Earlier—days before—he had killed the men without mercy because to them he was a beast, and to him they were enemies of his race.

This was different. This man was a friend, unmistakably, unalterably. And there was more to it. They were two intelligent beings facing each other; and though the ezwal realized it only vaguely, he felt the kinship that exists between all intelligence once it is in communication.

He understood in a remote part of his mind the kind of antagonism that can exist between intelligent life forms. But his emotional development had not reached that point. And so, only the feeling of communication and kinship was ascendant.

Then Jamieson spoke aloud, in a low, resonant voice, and his words were meaningless to the ezwal but his thoughts were crystalline. "I am your friend, and I stand between you and certain death. Not because these men are your enemies, but because you will not let them be your friends.

"You can kill me easily, and I know that you do not consider your life important. But think of this: while we stand here, some ezwal on your home planet may be killing a human being, or being killed by one. And though we are a vast distance away, it is now in your power to decide whether such senseless killing will stop soon or continue for a long time.

"Do not think that I am offering you an easy, cowardly way out. The task of bringing ezwals and human beings into mutual harmony will not be a simple one. There will be many members of both races to convince of the truth. You will encounter many of mine who regard all beings very much different from themselves as animals and automatically beneath them. Such ignorant people do not control this world, but they may try your patience before we are done. Many of your own race will regard you as a traitor, at first, simply because they do not understand the truth any better than these men behind me here. The job of making them understand may be long and hard, but it can be done with your help. And it can start now."

Calmly Jamieson turned his back on the ezwal and faced the others. Commander McLennan looked dumfounded as Jamieson said, "Commander, will you please ask one of your men to get my medical kit from the control room? Our guest has a badly injured foot which needs attention."

McLennan blinked. Speechless, he caught the eye of one of his men and nodded. The man started for the control room.

"But you will observe," added Jamieson, "that he also has five other sound ones, so don't anyone make the mistake of trying to shut the door until we are sure he is willing."

The ezwal had been standing like a statue, the torture of indecision in his mind increasing with every passing moment. Already, by delaying so long, he had made the very impression on those present that he had staked everything to avoid—the indelible idea that here was a creature of intelligence.

The man who had gone to the control room returned with a small case and handed it to Jamieson, reaching a little in order to do so. Jamieson turned and set the case in the doorway between them. Once more he looked the ezwal in the eye.

"If you will lie down so I can get at that foot of yours," he said soberly, "I think I can do something for it."

The man's mind seemed wide open. This was the final showdown, and there was no slightest pretense about that—but he also, sincerely, wanted to help.

Even as the ezwal made his decision, he realized it had been inevitable. He felt only a great relief as he lay down and extended his sore foot.

XIV

THE GREAT CITY was visible now in the mist ahead. The city of the Ship. Earlier, Jamieson had phoned his wife from the plane, and that was her first knowledge that he was back. But she had hurriedly brought Diddy from the Play Square, and there had been an excited three-way conversation.

Their eagerness made him feel guilty, for he should have called her on his return. He had been four and a half months absent in space and he knew it would disturb her if she discovered he had spent additional weeks saving the life of an ezwal cub. He had already decided not to tell her.

Sitting now in his plane seat, Jamieson shook his head at the problems which confronted men and women of this age. Everything—family life, child care, love and personal desires—came second to the all-consuming demand of the century-long war with the Rull enemy. In less than an hour he would be home. There would be kisses intermingled with tears; for Veda was a woman of intense emotion. For a while, he knew, she would match his ardor; then for a time her demand would exceed his; and then the flame would gradually dim. Meanwhile, he would quickly become immersed in his great administrative position, which he deserted less and less often these days. He could count on the fingers of one hand the kind of problem that would take him from his desk. One was the kind of idea that had come to him about the ezwals.

Two facts had made that a matter for the head of the Science Department. No one else would have generated any enthusiasm about ezwals possibly being intelligent, and so he could not trust anyone to take seriously the project of capturing one or more of the beings. And, secondly, the fact that it had to do with Carson's Planet, one of the three pivots of man's defense against the Rulls. Under such circumstances, to have a new thought about ezwals had made action mandatory. There were a few other possibilities, but for the most part, there was no necessity for him to do "field" work any more.

And so, one day, not long after the young ezwal was captured, he sat in his office conducting an interview important enough to require the attention of the "boss." It was a top-priority interview, but nothing that would take him from Earth.

"Here!" said Trevor Jamieson. He put the point of his pencil down in the center of a splotch of green on the map before him. He looked up at the wiry man opposite him. "Right here, Mr. Clugy," he said, "is where the camp will be built."

Ira Clugy leaned forward and gazed at the spot. He seemed puzzled, and there was the beginning of irritation in his voice as he asked, "Why that particular spot?"

"It's very simple," said Jamieson. It disturbed him to treat a mature man as if he were a child. But the Rull-human war required administrators to play many games. "The whole purpose of the project," he continued, "is to get fluid from the progeny of these Mira lymph beasts for our laboratories—quickly and in quantity. This forest area is their main habitat. Therefore the camp should be located in it, for quickest results."

He could not help but approve of Clugy's exasperated reaction. He would be lucky not to receive a punch in the nose, Jamieson thought ruefully. The spaceman's oversized hands clenched in an effort at self-control, and he swallowed hard.

"Mr. Jamieson," he said quietly, "as you know, we have already made a preliminary survey. There's never been a forest like that in Man's experience. It swarms with the young of the lymph beast and with a thousand other deadly creatures." He stood up and bent over the topographical map of the Mira planet. "Now here," he said briskly, "in this mountain country it's bad enough, but the animal and plant life can be fought off, and the climate is bearable. We can situate there, shuttle back and forth in alternating shifts and get all the juice you want. And more cheaply, too, when you consider the cost of clearing and maintaining a forest site."

It was as sensible an analysis as Jamieson had heard. If Clugy were Rull-controlled, he was doing very well indeed. Jamieson knew that Clugy's reactions were being studied by a psychotechnic team in another room, where this scene was being projected. If he struck a false note, a warning light not visible to Clugy would show on the panel on Jamieson's desk. But the panel remained dark.

Jamieson persisted: "For reasons which we are not free to discuss, the lymph fluid is too vital to worry about the expense of obtaining it. We must have it and have it fast. Besides, the contract, if you get it, will be cost-plus—subject to our audit, of course. Therefore—"

"Hang the cost!" said Clugy, and he rasped the words. "I shouldn't have mentioned it! What really matters is exposing several hundred good men to unnecessary hazards."

"I disagree that the hazards are unnecessary," said Jamieson. He was pushing hard now, anxious to force a crisis. "And I take full responsibility for my decision."

Clugy sank slowly back into his chair. The tan of

many suns on his face was matched by a flush of anger. But again he visibly held himself in check.

"Listen, Mr. Jamieson," he said finally, "there is a small mountain—a large hill—on the edge of that jungle area. It's mentioned in my report. It's not what I'd call a good site but it lacks some of the worst features of the lowlands. If the government insists on a camp close to the source of supply—or, rather, if *you* insist, since you have full authority—we'll build it on that hill. But I'm telling you straight: that's as close as I'll ask my men to stay, if it costs me the contract."

Jamieson was distinctly unhappy now. He was conscious of how irrational he must seem to this practical engineer. But his pencil point went back to the middle of the green splotch and pressed there firmly. "Here," he said with finality.

That was the straw. Clugy's wiry body uncoiled from his chair like a steel spring. His first came down on Jamieson's desk hard enough to make it vibrate.

"Damn it all," he raged, "you're like a lot of other swivel-chair tin gods I've met! You've sat behind that desk for so long you've lost touch with reality, but you figure you can maintain a reputation for being tough just by ordering everything done the hardest possible way—even if it endangers the lives of better men than yourself! Brother, if I could just put you down for five minutes in that green hell right where the point of your pencil is resting, then we'd see where you wanted the camp built!"

It was the outburst Jamieson had been working for, and still there was no warning signal. He felt relieved. It remained now to end the interview without revealing that it had been a test.

"Really, Mr. Clugy," he said soberly, "I'm surprised that you introduce personalities into this purely governmental affair."

Clugy's stare was unflinching, though his expression of fury had abated to a black scowl. "Mr. Jamieson," he said harshly, "a man who would send others into an impossible situation on a mere whim has already brought in the personal element. If that's where you want the camp built, you can build it there yourself. I'm ordering my crew back to Earth. To hell with the contract—cost-plus or any other kind."

Clugy turned on his heel and strode toward the door. Jamieson made no attempt to stop him. The test was not quite complete. The clincher would be whether Clugy would go through with his threat to call his men back from Mira 23 and thus withdraw all claim to the contract. That was something the Rulls would never do —relinquish control, through Clugy, of a top-priority project like the lymph-fluid one—no matter if the camp had to be built on a volcano. They wouldn't conceivably carry a pretense of concern for human personnel so far as that.

Trevor Jamieson set a dial and flipped a switch on the desk panel. A screen lighted, showing a group of three men. This was the psychotechnic team which had been observing Clugy as minutely as a variety of ultrasensitive detection instruments would allow them.

"Well," said Jamieson. "Looks as if Clugy's clean, wouldn't you say, gentlemen?"

One of the men smiled. "That fit of temper was pure Clugy. I bet on him."

"If I can win him back into the fold," said Jamieson grimly. "Let's hope the Rulls don't get to him before he leaves for Mira."

That, unfortunately for mankind, was the disastrous part. They could never be sure, particularly here on man's home planet. Nowhere in the human-controlled sector of the galaxy was Rull spy activity so well established as on Earth itself, despite the most intensive and unremitting counterespionage. The reasons for this situation went back a hundred years, to the fateful time in human history when the first destroying Rull armada had come from beyond a region of dark obscuring matter stretched across one arm of the galaxy.

A thousand planetary systems were lost to them before humanoids could mobilize their fleets and counterattack in sufficient force to halt the advance. For a few years the far-flung battlefront held fairly steady, the Rulls' cold, ruthless tenacity being met by man's sheer, selfless valiance, the older, more evenly balanced science of the enemy being offset by the matchless creativity of the human mind under stress.

Then the Rull tide began to move inexorably forward again, as one after another of human military plans miscarried, and some of the most secret strategy was anticipated. This seemed to mean only one thing. Spies were getting information for the enemy.

The ability of Rulls to control light with the cells of their bodies was not even suspected until one day a "man" was blasted while attempting to escape after being caught rifling the secret files of the Research Council. As the human image dissolved into a wormlike shape with numerous reticulated legs and arms, human beings had their first inkling of the fantastic danger that threatened.

Within a few hours, armed cars and airships were combing every city and every byway of a thousand planets, turning citizens out of all buildings and using radar to silhouette their true shapes.

A hundred thousand Rull spies were found and executed in that one roundup on Earth alone. But since that time the search had never ceased. The Rulls had soon developed a supplemental device which enabled them to foil all but the most complex interlocking radar detector systems.

And thus, decade by decade, the summing up showed the Rulls were gaining. They were a hardy, silicon-fluorine life form, almost immune to chemicals and bacteria that affected men. The compelling problem for man had been to find an organism in his own part of the galaxy that would enable him to experiment for bacteriological warfare.

The progeny of the lymph beast was that organism. Even Ira Clugy had been misled regarding the fluid's purpose. He had accepted the idea that it had something to do with air-regeneration plants for large battleships. It was hoped the Rulls had acquired the same false idea.

Jamieson's thoughts were interrupted by the buzz of the intercom from the outer office. He excused himself to the group of psychotechnicians and switched the screen over to the face of his secretary.

"Mr. Caleb Carson calling," said the young woman.

"Put him on," said Jamieson.

The secretary nodded, and her image on the screen was replaced by the serious, intelligent-looking visage of a dark-haired young man. Caleb Carson was the grandson of the discoverer of Carson's Planet and an accomplished student of that primitive world, and of the human-ezwal conflict.

"Ready," he said.

Jamieson felt a surge of eagerness. "I'll be right over," he said, and broke the connection.

To his secretary he said, "I going over to the Research Center. If any report comes through on Ira Clugy relay it to me there."

"Yes, sir."

As he left his office, Jamieson congratulated himself once more for the brain storm that had made him appoint the grandson of the founder of Carson's Planet as trainer for the young ezwal. If anyone had a stake in the success of a plan that would stabilize the situation on Carson's Planet it was young, brilliant Caleb Carson.

Jamieson took an elevator to the roof hangar where his aerocar was parked. Two armed guards at the hangar doorway nodded politely, then proceeded to frisk him thoroughly and check his identifcation. Jamieson submitted patiently to this laying on of hands; it was the surest, simplest way of apprehending Rull agents, and the government offices of this building contained much classified information in their files.

His aerocar, along with several others, was parked on the open door beside the hangar. As he came up to it his eyes were attracted by a peculiar tracery of lines on a small area of siliceous material that made up the surface.

Jamieson blinked, then shook his head. There was an odd sensation in it, a sense of heat, and then—once more he squeezed his eyes shut, but the image of the tracery remained as if the pattern matched some natural pathway inside his brain.

He found himself in the aerocar; and he was guiding it up and toward a distant building before he thought, What in hell was that?

He was still nervous, and strangely frantic, as he put his small craft down on the roof of a tall building. Absently, still introspective, still puzzled and disturbed, he stopped and waited for the parking attendant to bring him his ticket. As the attendant came toward him, he noticed that it was a new man, one he had not seen before. And then, looking around, he noticed something completely astonishing.

This building was *not* the Research Center!

Not only that, but it bore no particular resemblance to the center. Disconcerted, he turned to the attendant to make an apology. He froze. The man's hand held, not a ticket, but a shiny weapon. Jamieson felt a cold gust of gas in his face and a strangling constriction in his throat. Then there was blackness.

XV

THE NEXT sense impression to reach his consciousness was the thick, rancid odor of rotting vegetation, at once familiar and strange. He stayed as he was, eyes closed, body very still, forcing his breath into the slow, deep pattern of a sleeper. He was lying on something that felt like a canvas cot. It sagged in the middle but was reasonably comfortable. His thoughts became analytical. Was he a victim of . . . Rulls? Or was this personal? As chief scientist for the Interstellar Military Commission, he had in his time offended many bold and dangerous individuals, on Earth and other planets. Ira Clugy? He wondered. He was certainly the latest of the offended individuals. But would Clugy kidnap a government official for the sole purpose of clinching an argument? It seemed impossible. Jamieson's mind leaped back to the bizarre pattern of lines that had snatched his attention. A new form of mind control? Even as he had the thought, he realized that further speculation would solve nothing.

Jamieson opened his eyes. He was staring up through dense foliage at a blue-green, glowing sky. He grew abruptly aware that he was perspiring copiously, and that it was almost unbearably hot, and that the place was alive with machine sounds. He sat up, swung his legs off the cot, and slowly climbed to his feet. He then noticed that he was dressed in a fine-mesh suit that encased him from head to foot. It was the kind of hunting outfit used on primitive planets that swarmed with hostile life of every description. He saw that his cot was at the edge of a clearing that was in process of being created. Graders, bulldozers and a score of other road-building monsters were at work. Plastic huts were going up to his right. Some were already erected. If this were Mira 23, then Clugy's office would already be in operation.

It was Clugy—he now accepted that. There could be no other explanation. And, by God, Clugy had better be prepared to explain.

As he started toward the line of huts, Jamieson noticed that the green tint of the sky was the result of an energy screen. He detected the screen by the slight blurring of the outline of the treetops beyond it. The observation ended any confusion that remained, for the greenish effect was due to the screen's absorption of the lower visible frequencies from the oversized red giant sun, which now blazed so whitely at the zenith of the screen. Mira the red, the wonderful!

Twice, as Jamieson walked, discing machines harumphed past him sowing their insect poison, and he had to step gingerly over the loose earth. In its early stages the poison was as unfriendly to human beings as it was to anything else. The upturned soil glittered with long, black shiny worms writhing feebly, with the famous red Mira bugs that shocked their victims with electric currents, and with other *things* that he did not recognize. He reached the area of the huts, walked on, and came presently to a sign which read:

MERIDAN SALVAGE CO.
IRA CLUGY
CHIEF ENGINEER

Jamieson strode into the hut. A youth of perhaps twenty sat at a desk inside, looking annoyingly cool and alert to the perspiring Jamieson.

"Where's Ira Clugy?" demanded Jamieson without preliminaries.

The lad looked him over without any particular surprise. "Who are you? I don't remember seeing you around here before."

"My name is Trevor Jamieson. That mean anything to you?"

The youth didn't bat an eye. "The name does. That's the wheel assigned to this project by the Military Commission. You couldn't be Jamieson. He's not a field man."

Jamieson ignored the objection. "You must be Peter Clugy."

"How did you know that?" The boy looked steadily at Jamieson, then added, "Knowing my name doesn't prove you're Trevor Jamieson. How *did* you get here anyhow? There hasn't been a ship for five days."

"Five days?" echoed Jamieson, shocked.

The young man nodded.

Five days, thought Jamieson. And the trip from Earth would have taken seven or eight. Could Ira Clugy have kept him unconscious and concealed all that time without the nephew's knowing it?

"Where," demanded Jamieson simply, "is your uncle?"

Peter Clugy shook his head. "I don't think I ought to tell you that, without knowing who you are or how you got here. But I'll call him." He picked up the phone from the desk and pressed a button on an adjacent panel. After a moment came the faint sound of a voice on the line. It became exclamatory as Peter Clugy imparted the message. Then Jamieson was startled to hear the lad describing him personally.

"Above average height, somewhat bushy sandy hair, with a pronounced widow's peak, very dark eyes, wide forehead, prominent features—" Peter Clugy paused as the voice on the line spoke briefly, then said, "Okay, but you'd better bring a couple of men with you, just in case." He hung up and turned to Jamieson. "My uncle says you *could* be Jamieson, from the description. *Or* a Rull posing as Jamieson."

Jamieson smiled and stood up. He stepped forward, extending his hand. "Here—I'll prove I'm not a Rull, at least. Shake hands."

Peter Clugy's hand was palm down on the desk. He moved it just enough to reveal a small but deadly blaster beneath it. "Keep your distance," he said evenly. "Time enough for tests when my uncle gets here."

Jamieson stared at him a moment, then shrugged. He turned his back and sauntered to the doorway.

"Come away from there," said young Clugy sharply. "Better sit down where I can watch you."

Jamieson ignored him and stood looking out at the rather remarkable panorama beyond. In coming to this hut he had been too intent on his personal problem to notice the sweeping view from the campsite. This must be the compromise location Clugy had suggested during their bitter discussion back on Earth. This hill rose a thousand feet above the floor of the jungle, but not too sharply. Now that most of the growth was cleared from its crest it afforded a magnificent view of the vast, shining forest below, whose green splendor reached all the way to the dimly seen mountains based below the horizon.

He saw the glint of rivers, the sparkling colors of strange trees; and, as he looked, the old, perennial thrill stirred within him, a feeling of exaltation in contemplating this universe of fabulous planets and of wondrous stars, like the famed Mira sun above him.

The sight of three armed men crossing the clearing toward him reminded him abruptly of the urgency of the moment. The wiry figure in front would be that of Ira Clugy. As he came close enough for recognition, his deeply tanned face took on what Jamieson would have sworn was a look of honest bewilderment.

Ira Clugy said nothing until, at his gesture, the others had "frisked" Jamieson and established his humanness beyond question. Then: "Just one more thing, Mr. Jamieson. I wouldn't insist on it if you hadn't shown up here in such a mysterious fashion." The engineer took a pen from the desk and held it out. "Please sign your name on this pad so I can compare it with some papers in our file which bear your signature."

When that was established, Clugy said, "All right, then, Mr. Jamieson, I'd like to ask you one question: How did you get here?"

Jamieson smiled grimly. "Believe it or not, I came to this office to ask *you* that same question." There was, he decided suddenly, nothing to be gained by withholding anything.

He told Clugy all of the story that he knew, from the time he had left his office in Solar City until his arrival on this planet. He withheld nothing—not even his suspicions of Clugy.

At this, Ira Clugy was ironically amused. "You don't know me very well," he said. "I could have cheerfully punched you in the nose when I talked to you in your office. But kidnaping's not my style." Clugy went on to outline the events following his angry parting from Jamieson. He had gone directly to the Spaceman's Club and radioed his crew on Mira 23 to pack up and come home. He was submersing his choler at the club bar when he was approached by a government agent who explained the reason for the difficult session with Jamieson. Mollified, Clugy countermanded the order to his crew. Next morning he signed the contract and began loading additional men and equipment aboard one of his salvage ships. Two days later he departed for Mira 23. Clugy finished, "You can radio Earth to verify what I've told you."

"I must radio Earth anyway," he told Clugy, "and I'll check your story as a matter of course, though I really believe you. But far more important is to get a big ship here as fast as we can. What happened to me was no accident and we're not through with it."

The radio shack was not far away and readily identifiable by the cone-shaped configuration of rings above it which formed the subspace antenna. The radio operator peered out from behind the control panel as they entered. There was a worried look on his face.

"Mr. Clugy! I was just going to call you. It's the Mc-Laurin condenser again. It's burned out."

Clugy looked at the man with a grim expression. "I'm afraid, Landers, I'm going to have to put you under arrest."

The remark seemed to stun the young man. Jamieson was also surprised, and said so.

Clugy said, "Doctor, this is the third and last condenser. It'll be six days before another ship arrives, and they of course will have a stock of spares. Meanwhile, we are out of radio communication."

The appalling significance of that instantly justified the arrest. In a flash, Jamieson sized up the situation. There were four of them here in the room: the two Clugys, the radio operator and himself. Outside, the roar of machinery nullified the possibility of any human-made sound being heard.

Young Peter Clugy interrupted his train of thought, placed a blaster on the table beside him. "Here, sir; you cover him while I give him the test."

Jamieson snatched the gun, relieved to have a weapon again. He stepped back and waved the younger Clugy forward. Beside him, Ira Clugy also pulled his blaster.

They stood watchful, as the radio operator extended his hand.

After the handshake, Clugy's nephew seemed relieved as he turned to Jamieson and said, "He's human, sir."

The atmosphere in the shack grew less tense. "Where," Jamieson asked, "is the nearest available transmitter?"

"At the uranium mining camp, nine hundred miles south," Clugy replied, and added, "You can have one of our aerocars and leave right away. In fact, I'll take you myself."

Young Peter Clugy immediately started off toward a group of small ships standing in a row across the clearing. "I'll bring you one," he called over his shoulder.

Minutes later they were in the air, the dense, waxen-green forest sliding rapidly northward a thousand feet below. Peter Clugy had elected to pilot the ship for them; at the moment, he was expertly setting the automatic controls for the prescribed course.

Ira Clugy sat staring silently out the window, apparently in no mood to talk. Jamieson didn't blame him—it was time to straighten out his own thoughts on a few matters.

The purpose of the Rulls, he told himself, is to delay or block altogether the procurement of lymph fluid. That premise should be the key to the whole situation. But why would they arrange to trap him by their bizarre, mind-seizing line patterns and bring him here, apparently on one of their own ships? He shuddered at the thought of being in their alien custody during the long trip through space.

And why did they let me live? There was only one reasonable explanation. It would not be sufficiently damaging to the project merely to kill the administrator, who could be replaced in due course. There must be a deeper plan, one involving Ira Clugy, undoubtedly, which would be calculated to hold up the entire operation for some time.

Apparently, the plan required that Jamieson's presence be established here. That was simple enough. All they had to do was to set him down in the camp, probably before dawn, and he had taken care of the rest of it himself, quite naturally.

Jamieson felt a sudden uneasiness. Everything else he had done had been quite natural also, *and quite predictable.* What was more natural than that he—and Ira Clugy, too, for that matter—would be here in this small craft on their way across nine hundred miles of desolation toward the nearest subspace radio station, now that the one in the camp had failed. Yes, quite predictable, from the viewpoint of some agent who had cleverly sabotaged the subspace radio but who didn't know about the patrol ship above the atmosphere.

Jamieson got to his feet. The mining camp must be contacted immediately, before it was too late!

It was then, glancing quickly around the horizon, that he saw another ship approaching. Although he had more than half expected it, the sight sent a thrill of alarm along his nerves. It was larger and faster than their own ship, and probably armed. At that angle and speed it would overtake them in two or three minutes!

Jamieson turned hastily toward the radio panel—and stopped. Peter Clugy stood before it, his face expressionless, but holding in his hand the same small blaster he had displayed earlier. It was aimed at Jamieson's stomach.

There was a gasp from Ira Clugy. "Peter, you young fool! Have you lost your mind?" He got out of his seat and stepped forward as the menacing blaster swung around toward him. "Here, give me that thing!"

Jamieson put out a restraining arm in front of the

older man. "I only hope your nephew hasn't lost his life," he said, trying to keep his voice calm. "This is not Peter Clugy—nor any other human being."

XVI

IN JAMIESON'S MIND several things fell suddenly into place. Peter Clugy's refusal to shake hands on the pretense that *he* thought *Jamieson* might be a Rull. And the first thing he had noticed about young Clugy was his unnatural physical coolness in this superheated, humid climate—obvious now. And since it was Peter Clugy who had "established" by handshake the humanness of the radio operator, *that* individual must also be . . . Rull.

Jamieson studied the "youth" closely. There was no flaw in the human image that he could detect. He had to admit the perfection. It was apparently an inflexible rule that a disguise never be relaxed in the presence of human beings. Jamieson approved wholeheartedly. He had always found the sight of their wormlike, multi-appendaged bodies upsetting.

Ira Clugy had recovered from his initial shock. He glared at the Rull. "What have you done with my nephew?" he demanded. He started forward threateningly.

Jamieson held him back. "Careful, my friend, He doesn't need the blaster. He could destroy us with a bolt of high-frequency stuff that he can control with his body cells."

The Rull said nothing but extended what appeared to be a human hand toward the control panel and pulled a lever. At once, the ship began to sink toward the green forest below.

A glance around told Jamieson that the other ship had come in close and was descending with them. A minute later, brush crackled beneath the hull as they came to rest on the ground. Strangely, the other aerocar did not land but remained hovering a few feet above the ground a dozen yards away, its purring underjets automatically supplying just enough to lift to offset its slight residual weight.

Could the purpose be to leave no trace of the other ship's presence here? As he watched, the ship's two occupants, both human in appearance, both undoubtedly Rulls, jumped from its doorway to the ground and started across the intervening space. What startled Jamieson was their apparent disregard of the ground over which they passed. It was startling because this was the heart of the Green Forest, alive with the young of the lymph beast!

Perhaps the Rulls didn't really know what the purpose was of Clugy's work. Perhaps this was just a routine spy operation to sabotage a human project. Not knowing, they might well have confused the adult lymph beast with the progeny. The parent was harmless. The young attacked anything that moved. If it ceased moving before they reached it, they forgot about it instantly. Utterly indiscriminate, they struck at leaves drifting in the wind, the waving branch of a tree, even moving water. Millions of the snakelike things died every month making insensate attacks on inanimate objects that had moved for one reason or another. But some, inevitably, survived the first two months of their existence and changed into their final form.

In the development of the lymph beast, Nature had achieved one of her most fantastic balancing acts. The ultimate shape of the lymph beast was a hard-shelled beehivelike construction *that could not move*. It was hard to go far into the Green Forest without stumbling across one of these structures. They were everywhere —on the ground and in trees, on hillsides and in valleys; wherever the young monster happened to be at the moment of the change, there the adult settled. The final stage was short but prolific. The hive lived entirely on the food it had stored up as a youngster. Being bisexual, it spent its brief existence in a sustained ecstasy of procreation. The young, however, were not discharged from it. They incubated inside and promptly began eating at the vitals of the parent. This stopped the process of reproduction, but by this time there were many of them. They also ate each other, but as the shell softened and fell apart from the action of their secretions, a certain proportion would reach comparative safety outside.

Jamieson's thoughts ended as the Rull-image of Peter Clugy flipped a switch, opening the door of the aerocar, and gestured with the blaster.

"Get ouside, you two!"

Reluctantly, they preceded their captor to the ground outside, where the other two Rulls now stood waiting. The heat was suffocating. On Earth, in an almost rainless climate like this, the vegetation would be brown and desiccated; here, the grassy glade and surrounding forest were almost artificial-looking in their waxen greenness.

The images of all three Rulls wavered slightly, one after another. "They're talking it over," Jamieson explained to Clugy in a low voice. "Apparently it's difficult to communicate with light waves and maintain a perfect image."

The image of Peter Clugy turned abruptly toward Ira and gestured. "All right, you can leave now."

Ira Clugy looked blank. "Leave?"

"Yes. Get back in your ship and take off. Go to your camp or wherever you please. But don't come back here again today!"

Jamieson felt as baffled as Ira Clugy looked. Clugy seemed to brace himself. "Nothing doing," he said flatly. "If Mr. Jamieson stays, I stay."

The likeness of Peter Clugy hesitated. Then, "But why? We know that you have a personal dislike for this man."

"Maybe I did once, but—" Ira Clugy stopped. His face twisted with renewed fury as the full implication of the Rull's remark sank in. "So you know about that! That means my nephew was dead—and you were taking his place—even back on Earth!"

Jamieson laid a restraining hand on the engineer's shoulder, or the man would surely have lunged at the Rull.

The Rull said, "Your nephew is not dead. He is—here."

Moving to the aft storage compartment of the ship beside which they were standing, the Rull slid open the hatch. Inside lay a motionless figure identical in appearance with the one which had opened the door.

"He should remain unconscious for several hours," said the Rull. "He was surprisingly resistant to paralysis. But he will recover. It was only this morning, however, in your camp, that I took his place. That has not been necessary before, in order to find out what we needed to know."

Jamieson could well believe that. Ira Clugy had undoubtedly broadcast his feelings sufficiently at the Spaceman's Club following the memorable altercation in Jamieson's office. Also, all personnel had been carefully checked for humanness before embarking for this planet.

The Rull appeared to be conferring with his fellow agents. They had evidently not planned for Clugy's opposition.

It was at that instant, while his mind was straining to fit together the pieces of the puzzling actions of the Rulls, that a movement in the grass caught Jamieson's attention. It was some distance away, and he could see only a series of shadows. But he felt an inner tremble of terrible fear.

Dark forest of Mira, he thought shakily. Alive with the young of the lymph beast . . .

The brief conference among the Rulls ended and the replica of Peter Clugy spoke to Ira. "It is not necessary for you to take the ship back yourself. I will take you within a short distance of the camp and leave you and the ship there. Now get in!"

Ira Clugy's jaw set. "And what happens to Mr. Jamieson?"

"We leave him here," replied the Rull. "It will be dark in an hour. Before you can possibly get back here and find him, he will be dead.

Jamieson was thinking, The administrator dead, the field engineer freed. Why? Suddenly he got it. Of course. People would remember Clugy's wild talk about subjecting the project administrator to Mira's environment. And instantly the chief of field operations would be under suspicion of murder, and deliveries of lymph fluid might be seriously delayed.

It was a bold yet fairly simple purpose. And it emphasized that the Rull did not know the importance of the project they were attacking.

Somewhere a Rull spy center had been advised of this human activity on Mira 23 and had detached a group of spies to handle it. The individuals involved, lacking full information, were proceeding on a typical Rull plan with the usual Rull bravery.

Jamieson glanced from the corner of his eye at the advancing line of what could only be the lymph progeny. The irregular line was now only thirty or forty feet away, and at one point he caught a glimpse of a writhing, mottled gray shape. In a minute the creatures would be all around them.

Jamieson waited not an instant longer. He had to trust that his analysis of the Rull plan was correct, and he had to use his great knowledge of the Rull enemy. In two steps he was over to Clugy.

"You get into that ship," he said in a loud voice. "No reason why both of us should die."

In a whisper he added, "We're surrounded by lymph. I'll save myself by holding still. Get!" He gave Clugy a shove, sending him staggering toward the aerocar. Clugy recovered his balance, hesitated, then dived into the aerocar and, without waiting for the Rulls, took off.

Jamieson merely took note. He was running toward a near edge of jungle. They won't kill me, he told himself. That would spoil their plan.

If he could hold their attention a few seconds more . . .

Before he could have another thought, there was a crackling in the air about him, and every nerve in his body seemed to gather into a knot. Completely helpless, he fell like a stick, his left shoulder crunching against the ground.

He did not lose consciousness, but a moment passed before his head cleared sufficiently to realize that what he had wanted to happen had happened. One of the Rulls had reached him with a discharge of paralyzing energy. He wondered whether he had broken any bones in his left shoulder or arm, but there was no way to tell. They were completely numb, like the rest of him. A terrifying thought leaped to his mind: What if one of the lymph things had struck as he hit the ground and was even now feeding on his vitals! Would the only indication be a fading of consciousness as his lifeblood ebbed away?

A brilliant, soundless flash of light interrupted that grin speculation. Then there were a whole series of flashes in quick succession. Their source was out of Jamieson's limited range of vision, but he could guess what was happening.

Minutes went by. The flashes of light diminished to an occasional flicker. The smell of ozone reached his nostrils. His eyes were already smarting with it, but he could not close them.

A moment later he wished fervently that he could. Into the lower edge of his field of vision, as he lay on his side, an indescribably hideous small head moved and poised a matter of inches from his chin. It was one of the lymph progeny, and although Jamieson could feel nothing, he could tell from the position of the head that the creature was in the act of crawling over his body!

The fearful little head moved on, dipping out of his sight but leaving on Jamieson's mind an indelible impression of its numerous tiny eyes, like bright pinheads, and the yellow, sucking mouth studded with concentric rings of thornlike teeth.

Endless minutes passed. Perhaps they had already left. Suddenly the ground seemed to move away from under his head, and he relized he was being lifted from behind. He went up so rapidly that his first thought was that more than one person must be doing the lifting, but a moment later he found himself hanging over the shoulder of Ira Clugy.

The wiry engineer was simply wasting no time. He had landed the ship as close as possible, and he now hustled Jamieson into it.

Before the hatch closed, Jamieson caught a glimpse of the three Rulls lying in the grass fifty feet away. The humanoid images they had projected in life were gone, and their natural wormlike, multi-appendaged forms were revealed. Here and there, the dark bodies showed a glossy sheen, evidence that some of the light-controlling cells were still alive. But they were dead. There had been plenty of time for the little monsters to bury themselves in their victims completely.

XVII

"WHAT NAME?" Jamieson asked, amused.

He was homeward bound from fabulous Mira 23, and on instantaneous radio contact with Earth.

Caleb Carson replied, "He wanted your name; then, when the Play Square said it would be confusing, he settled for Ephraim."

Jamieson leaned back in the special chair used to insulate individuals transmitting with the McLaurin tube. He smiled as he thought, So the young ezwal has accepted a name.

It was a milestone event. "What's in a name?" an ancient poet had written. "A rose by any other name," etc. But the poet in so saying made one of his few errors. For man, as he reached out into space, found races where individuals were not identified. Such races could not be "civilized."

Like all highly developed human beings who had a galactic outlook on life and the universe, Jamieson knew that for a hundred years "civilization" had had a slanted definition: a race was civilized to the extent it was able to participate in the defense against the Rulls.

From a practical point of view, no other definition could be considered.

"Ephraim," Jamieson echoed. "And the last name?"

"Jamieson. The Play Square allowed that."

"Well, a new addition to the family. Have you told my wife?"

"Yes. I called her. I'm afraid she was too worried about your disappearance to appreciate the honor."

Since he had already talked to Veda and relieved her anxiety, Jamieson was able to reply lightheartedly. And so they chatted across the years of miles. A decision grew out of the conversation: to prepare a muscle impregnating device that could transmit one *thought*: "My name is——" Each name would be different.

Millions of such devices would shortly be transported to Carson's Planet. There, borne by ships carrying mind-confusing machines, they would be fired through the skin and into the muscle of each ezwal sighted.

Such devices were made of material that would be absorbed into the blood stream after a time. But not before each impregnated ezwal knew that "My name is——"

Jamieson had no doubt that, if he appeared before the Galactic Convention with Ephraim and a mechanical telepathic device for identifying every ezwal on Carson's Planet, the convention would order the military council there to cooperate with him.

He broke that connection finally, satisfied; and then he called one of the government research assignment offices. There he talked to a neurologist about the "nerve" lines that had apparently hypnotized him. He described the location of the lines as best he could and then gave a surprisingly accurate—so it seemed to him —description of the structure of the lines themselves.

As he hung up, he thought, At least I'm getting things started.

A few days later he was back at his desk.

"You're wanted on the video," said Exchange.

Jamieson clicked on his machine. "Yes," he said, before the picture could form.

The woman whose face grew onto the videoplate looked agitated. "The Play Square just called me. Diddy has gone out to look for the sound."

"Oh," said Jamieson.

He studied her image. Hers was an exceptionally attractive face, clear-skinned, well-shaped, crowned with beautifully coiled black hair. At the moment it was not normal. Her eyes were widened, her muscles tensed and her hair slightly displaced. Marriage and motherhood had profoundly affected his beautiful sweetheart.

"Veda," he said sharply, "you're not letting it get you."

"But he's out there. And the whole area is said to be full of Rull spies." She shuddered as she spoke the name of the great enemy.

"The Play Square let him go, didn't it? It must think he's ready."

"But he'll be out all night."

Jamieson nodded slowly. "Look, darling, this had to happen. It's part of the process of growing up, and we've been expecting it since his ninth birthday last May." He broke off. "How about you going out and doing some shopping? That'll take your mind off him for the rest of the afternoon anyway. Spend"—he made a quick calculation, took another look at her face, and revised the initial figure upward—"what you like. On yourself. Now, goodbye, and don't worry."

He broke the connection hastily and climbed to his feet. For a long time he stood at the window staring down at The Yards. From his vantage point he could not see the "Way" or the ship; they were on the other side of the building. But the fairyland of streets and buildings that he could see enthralled him now as always. The Yards was a suburb of Solar City, and that massive metropolis in its artificial tropical setting was a vision that had no parallel in the human-controlled part of the Galaxy. Its buildings and its parks extended to every hazy horizon.

He drew his gaze back from the distance, back to the city proper of The Yards. Slowly, he turned from the window. Somewhere down there his nine-year-old son was exploring the world of the sound. Thinking about that or about the Rulls wouldn't do either Veda or himself the slightest good.

By the time the sky grew dark, Diddy Jamieson knew that the sound never ended. After wondering about it for his whole lifetime, or so it seemed, that was good to know. He'd been told that it ended somewhere "out there"—vaguely. But this afternoon he'd proved for himself that, no matter how far you went, the sound remained. The fact that his elders had lied to him about that did not disturb Diddy. According to his robot teacher, the Play Square, parents sometimes fibbed to test a fellow's ingenuity and self-reliance. This was obviously one of the fibs, which he had now disproved.

For all these years, the sound had been in his Play Square, and in the living room whether he was silent or trying to talk, and in the dining room making a rhythm out of the eating noises of Mom and Dad and himself—on those days he was permitted to eat with them. At night the sound crept into bed with him, and while he slept even in his deepest sleep, he could feel it throbbing in his brain. Yes, it was a familiar thing, and it was natural that he'd tried to find out if it stopped at the end of first one street and then another. Just how many streets he'd turned up and into and along, whether he'd gone east or west or north, was no longer clear. But wherever he'd gone, the sound had followed him. He had had dinner an hour ago at a little restaurant. Now it was time to find out *where* the sound began.

Diddy paused to frown over his location. The important thing was to figure out just where he was in relation to The Yards. He was figuring it by mentally calculating the number of streets between Fifth and Nineteenth, H and R, Center and Right, when he happened to glance up. There, a hundred feet away, was a man he'd first seen three blocks and ten minutes back.

Something about the movements of the man stirred a curious, unpleasant memory, and for the first time he saw how dark the sky had become. He began to walk casually across the road, and he was glad to notice that he was not afraid. His hope was that he would be able to get by the man, and so back to the more crowded Sixth Street. He hoped, also, that he was mistaken in his recognition of the man as Rull.

His heart sank as a second man joined the first, and the two started to cross the street to intercept him. Diddy fought an impulse to turn and run. Fought it, because if they were Rulls, they could move several times as fast as a man. Their appearance of having a humanlike body was an illusion which they could create by their control of light. It was that which had made him suspect the first of the two. In turning the corner the fellow's legs had walked *wrong*. Diddy could not remember how many times the Play Square had described such a possibility, but now that he had seen it, he realized that it was unmistakable. In the daytime the Rulls were said to be more careful with their illusions.

"Boy!"

Diddy slowed and looked around at the two men, as if seeing them for the first time.

"Boy, you're out on the streets rather late."

"This is my exploring night, sir," said Diddy.

The "man" who had spoken reached into his breast pocket. It was a curious gesture, not complete, as if in creating the illusion of the movement he hadn't quite

thought through the intricacies of such an action. Or
perhaps he was careless in the gathering darkness. His
hand came out and flashed a badge.

"We're Yard agents," he said. "We'll take you to the
Way."

He put the badge back into his pocket, or seemed to,
and motioned toward the brightness in the distance.

Diddy knew better than to resist.

Jamieson opened the door of his apartment for the
two police officers shortly after dinner. They wore plain
clothes, he recognized them instantly for what they were.

"Doctor Jamieson?" one of them asked.

"Yes?"

"Trevor Jamieson?"

He nodded this time, aware in spite of having just
eaten, of an empty sensation.

"You are the father of Dexter Jamieson, aged nine?"

Jamieson took hold of the doorjam. "Yes," he mumbled.

The spokesman said, "It is our duty, as required by
law, to inform you that at this moment your son is in
the control of two Rulls, and that he will be in grave
danger of his life for some hours to come."

Jamieson said nothing.

Quietly, the officer described how Diddy had been
taken over on the sidewalk. He added, "We've been
aware for some time that the Rulls have been concen-
trating in Solar City in more than usual numbers. Naturally, we haven't located them. As you may know, we
estimate their numbers on the basis of those we do
spot."

Jamieson did know, but he said nothing. The other
continued. "As you are probably also aware, we are
more interested in discovering the purpose of a Rull
ring than in capturing individuals. As with all Rull
schemes in the past, this one will probably prove to be

extremely devious. It seems clear that we have only witnessed the first step of an intricate plan. But now, is there any further information you wish?"

Jamieson hesitated. He was acutely conscious of Veda in the kitchen putting the dinner dishes into the dishwasher. It was vital that he get these policemen away before she found out what their mission was. Yet one question he had to ask.

"As I understand it, there'll be no immediate attempt to rescue Diddy?"

The officer said in a firm voice, "Until we have the information we want, this situation will be allowed to ripen. I have been instructed to ask you not to build up any hopes. As you know, a Rull can actually concentrate energy of blaster power with his cells. Under such circumstances, death can strike very easily." He broke off. "That's all, sir. You may call security headquarters from time to time if you desire further information. The police will not communicate with you again on their own initiative."

"Thank you," said Jamieson automatically. He closed the door and went with mechanical stolidity back to the living room.

Veda called from the kitchen, "Who was that, darling?"

Jamieson drew a deep breath. "Somebody looking for a man named Jamieson. They got the right name but the wrong man." His voice held steady for the words.

"Oh," said Veda.

She must have forgotten the incident at once, for she did not mention it again. Jamieson went to bed at ten o'clock. He lay there, conscious of a vague ache in his back and a sick feeling at the pit of his stomach. At one o'clock he was still awake.

XVIII

DIDDY KNEW he mustn't offer any resistance. He must make no attempt to frustrate any plans they might have. For years the Play Square had emphasized that. No young person, it had stated categorically, should consider himself qualified to judge how dangerous any particular Rull might be. Or how important the plan of a Rull spy ring. Assume that something was being done. And await whispered instructions.

Diddy was remembering all these things as he walked between the two Rulls, his short legs twinkling as he was hustled along faster than his normal pace. He was heartened by the fact that they had still not let him know their identity. They were still pretending.

The street grew much brighter. Ahead he could see the ship silhouetted against the blue-black sky. All the buildings that crowded The Way were giving off the sunlight they'd absorbed during the day. The hundred-story administration building glowed like a jewel in the shadow of a towering ship, and all the other buildings shone with an intensity of light that varied according to their sizes. With Diddy in tow, the two Rulls came to Cross 2. The Way itself was Cross 1.

They walked across the street and came to the barrier. The two Rulls paused in front of the eight-foot-wide band of fluted metal, with its constant suction effect, and stared down at the open ventilators.

A century before, when Rull and human being first

146

made contact, there had been concrete walls or electrified barbed-wire fences around defense plants and military areas. Then it was discovered that Rulls could deflect electric current, and that their tough skins were impervious to the sharp bite of barbed wire. Concrete was equally ineffective. The walls had a habit of crumbling in the presence of certain Rull-directed energies. And among workmen who arrived to repair them was usually a Rull who, by a process of image transference and murder, made his way inside. Armed patrols were all too frequently killed to a man, and their places taken by Rull impostors. The air-suction type of barrier was only a few years old. It extended all the way around The Yards. Human beings who tried to penetrate it died within about three minutes. It was one of man's top secrets.

Diddy seized on the hesitation of his two escorts. "Thanks for bringing me this far," he said. "I'll be able to manage now."

One of the spies laughed. It was reasonably like a human laugh, if you considered only the sound, but some vital, personal intonation was lacking. To Diddy's ears it sounded horrid.

The creature said, "You know, kid, you look like a pretty good sport. Just to show you that our hearts are in the right place, how'd you like to have a little fun—just for a minute?"

"Fun?" said Diddy.

"See that barrier there?"

Diddy nodded.

"Good. As we've already told you, we're security police—you know, anti-Rull. Of course we've got the problem on our minds all the time. You can see that, can't you?"

Diddy said that he could. He wondered what was coming.

"Well, the other day my friend and I were talking about our job, and we figured out a way by which a Rull might be able to cross the barrier. It seemed so silly that we thought we ought to test it before we reported it to the top brass—you know what I mean. If it turned out wrong, why, we'd look foolish. That's the test we want you to help us make."

No young person . . . must . . . attempt to frustrate any plans . . . of a Rull spy ring. The command, so often given by the Play Square, echoed in Diddy's mind. It seemed dreadfully clear that here was special danger, and yet it was not for him to judge or oppose. The years of training made that automatic now. He wasn't old enough to know.

"All you've got to do," said the Rull spokesman, "is walk between these two lines across the barrier and then walk back again."

The lines indicated were a part of the pattern of the fluted arrangement of the ventilators. Without a word of objection, Diddy walked across to the other side. Just for a moment, then, he hesitated, half minded to make a run for it to the safety of a building thirty feet away. He changed his mind. They could blast him before he could go ten feet. Dutifully, he came back, as he had been told to do.

A score of men were coming along the street. As they came near, Diddy and the two Rulls drew aside to let them pass. Diddy watched them hopefully. Police? He wondered. He wanted desperately to be sure that all that was happening was suspected.

The workmen trooped by, walked noisily across the barrier, and disappeared behind the nearest building.

"This way, kid," said the Rull. "We've got to be careful that we're not seen."

Diddy felt differently about that, but he followed. They went into a dark space between two buildings.

"Hold out your hand, kid."

He held it out, tense and scared. I'm going to die, he thought. And he had to fight back the tears. But his training won out, and he stood still as a needle-sharp pain jabbed his finger.

"Just taking a sample of your blood, kid. You see, the way we look at it, that suction system out there conceals high-powered micro-jets which send up bacteria to which the Rulls are vulnerable. Naturally, these micro-jets send up their shots of bacteria at about a thousand miles an hour, so fast that they penetrate your skin without your feeling them or their leaving a mark. And the reason the suction ventilators keep pulling in so much air is to prevent the bacteria from escaping into the atmosphere. And also the same culture of bacteria is probably used over and over again. You see where that leads us?"

Diddy didn't, but he was shocked to the core of his being. For this analysis sounded right. It *could* be bacteria that was being used against the Rulls. It was said that only a few men knew the nature of the defense projected by the innocent-looking barrier. Was it possible that at long last the Rulls were finding out?

He could see that the second Rull was doinging something in the shadowy region between the two buildings. There were little flashes of light. Diddy made a wild guess, and thought, He's examining my blood with a microscope to see how many dead anti-Rull bacteria are in it.

The Rull who had done all the talking so far said, "You know how it is, kid, you can walk across that barrier, and the bacteria that are squirted up from it die immediately in your blood stream. Our idea is this: There can be only one type of bacteria being sent up in any one area. Why? Because, when they're sucked down and sent back to the filter chambers so they can be removed from the air and used again, it would be too complicated if there were more than one type of bacteria. The highly virulent bacteria that thrive in a fluorine compound are almost as deadly to each other as to the organism which they attack. It's only when one type is present in enormously predominant amounts that it is dangerous to the Rulls. In other words, only one type at a time can kill a Rull.

"Obviously, if a Rull is shot full of immunization against that particular type of bacteria—why, kid, he can cross the barrier *at that point* as easily as you can, and he can do anything he wants to inside The Yards. You see how big a thing we're working on?" He broke off. "Ah, I see my friend has finished examining your blood. Wait here a moment." He moved off to where the other Rull was waiting. The conference, whatever its nature, lasted less than a minute.

The Rull came back. "Okay, kid, you can scoot along. Thanks a lot for helping us. We won't forget it."

Diddy could not believe his ears for a moment. "You mean that's all you want from me?" he asked.

"That's all."

As he emerged from the dark space between the two buildings, Diddy expected somehow that he would be stopped. But, though the two Rulls followed him out to the street, they made no attempt to accompany him as he started across it toward the barrier.

The Rull called after him, "There's a couple of other kids coming up the street; you might join them, and the bunch of you can look for the sound together."

Diddy turned to look, and as he did so, two boys came darting toward him yelling. "Last one over is a pig."

They had the momentum, and they were past him in a flash. As he raced after them, Diddy saw them hesitate, turn slightly, and then cross the barrier at a dead run over the ventilators which he had tested for the two Rull researchers. They waited for him on the other side.

"My name is Jackie," said one.

"And mine is Gil," said the second one. He added, "Let's stick together."

Diddy said, "My name is Diddy."

There were separate sounds, as the three of them walked, that drowned out *the* sound. Discordant noises. Whirring machines. An intricate pattern of clangorous hammerings. Rippling overtones from the molecular displacement of masses of matter. A rubber-wheeled train hummed toward them over the endless metal floor that carpeted The Yards and paused as its electronic eyes and ears sensed them. They stepped out of the way and it rushed past. A line of cranes lifted a hundred-ton metal plate onto an antigravity carrier. It floated away lightly, airily, into the blazing sky.

Diddy had never been on The Way at night before, and it would have been tremendously exciting if he had not been so miserable. The trouble was, he couldn't be sure. Were these two "boy" companions Rulls? So far they had done nothing that actually proved they were. The fact that they had crossed the barrier at the point where he had tested it for the two Rull "men" could have been a coincidence. Until he was sure, he dared not tell anyone what had happened. Until he was sure, he would have to go along with them, and even if they wanted him to do something, cooperate with them. That was the rule. That was the training. He had a picture in his mind of scores of such boys crossing the barrier at the test point. Even now they would be moving along The Way, free to do as they pleased.

The universe around The Way shivered with a concatenation of sounds. But nowhere that Diddy looked, no doorway into which he peered, no building he wandered through with wide, fascinated eyes—nowhere was there a sound that did not quickly fade away as he moved on. Not once did they come to anything that even faintly resembled a barrier-type ventilator. If there was any threat to wandering Rulls, it was not apparent. Doors stood wide open. He had hoped in a vague fashion that the atmosphere of some closed room would be deadly for the enemy and not for him. There were no closed rooms.

Worst of all, there was no sign of a human being who might conceivably protect him from the Rulls, or even suspect their presence. If only he could be sure that these two boys were Rulls. Or weren't. Suppose they carried some deadly weapon capable of causing tremendous damage to the ship?

They came to a building half a mile square. And Diddy grew suddenly hopeful. His companions offered no objection as he walked through a huge door onto a causeway. Below them was depth. From the causeway Diddy looked down at a dimly glowing world of huge, cubelike structures. The top of the highest cube was at least a quarter of a mile below the causeway, and it was blocked off by floor after floor of plastic, so limpedly transparent that only a gleam here and there revealed that there were many layers of hard, frustrating matter protecting the world above them from the enormous atomic piles in that colossal powerhouse.

As he approached the center of the causeway, Diddy saw, as he had a few moments before hopefully expected, that there was somebody in a little transparent structure that jutted out from the metalwork. A woman, reading. She looked up as the three of them came up, Diddy in the lead.

"Searching for the sound?" she asked in a friendly tone. She added, "Just in case you don't know—I'm a Sensitive."

The other boys were silent. Diddy said that he knew. The Play Square had told him about Sensitives. They could anticipate changes in the flow of an atomic pile. It had, he recalled, something to do with the way the calcium content in their blood was controlled. Sensitives lived to a very old age—around a hundred and eighty—not because of the jobs they had but because they could respond to the calcium rejuvenation processes.

The memory was only a background to his gathering disappointment. Apparently, she had no way of detecting the presence of a Rull. For she gave no sign. He'd better keep pretending that he was still interested in the sound, which was true in a way. He said, "Those dynamos down there would make quite a vibration, I guess."

"Yes, they would."

Diddy was suddenly intent. Impressed but not convinced. "Still, I don't see how it could make the big sound."

She said, "You all seem like nice boys. I'm going to whisper a clue into your ears. You first." She motioned to Diddy.

It seemed odd, but he did not hesitate. She bent down. "Don't be surprised," she whispered. "You'll find a very small gun under the overlapping edge of the metal sidewalk underneath the ship. Go down escalator seven and turn right. It's just on this side of a beam that has a big H painted on it. Nod your head if you understand."

Diddy nodded.

The woman continued swiftly. "Slip the gun into your pocket. Don't use it until you're ordered to. Good luck."

She straightened. "There," she said, "that should give you an idea." She motioned to Jackie. "You next."

The stocky boy shook his head. "I don't need no

clues," he said. "Besides, I don't want nobody whispering anything to me."

"Nor me either," said Gil.

The woman smiled. "You mustn't be shy," she said. "But never mind. I'll give you a clue anyway. Do you know what the word *miasma* means?" She spoke directly to Jackie.

"Mist."

"That's my clue, then. Miasma. And now, you'd better be getting along. The sun is due up a few minutes before six, and it's after two o'clock now."

She picked up her book and, when Diddy glanced back a few minutes later, she looked as if she were a part of the chair. She seemed scarcely alive, so still was she. But because of her, he knew the situation was as deadly as he had suspected. The great ship itself must be in danger. It was toward the ship that he headed.

XIX

TREVOR JAMIESON awakened suddenly to the realization that something had roused him, and that accordingly he must have slept. He groaned inwardly and started to turn over. If he only *could* sleep through this night. With a start he grew aware that his wife was sitting on the edge of the bed. He glanced at his illuminated watch. It was 2:22 A.M.

Oh, my gosh, he thought, I've got to get her back to bed.

"I can't sleep," said Veda. Her voice had a whimper in it, and he felt sick. For she was worrying like this about nothing definite. He pretended to be very thoroughly asleep.

"Darling."

Jamieson stirred, but that was all.

"Sweetheart."

He opened one eye. "Darling, please."

"I wonder how many other boys are out tonight."

Jamieson turned over. "Veda, what are you trying to do—keep me awake?"

"Oh, I'm sorry. I didn't mean to." Her tone was not sorry, and after a moment she seemed to have forgotten she'd spoken the words.

"My dear."

He didn't answer.

"Do you think we could find out?" she asked.

He'd intended to ignore further conversation, but his mind started to examine the possible meaning of what she'd said. He grew astonished at the meaninglessness of her words and woke up.

"Find out what?" he asked.

"How many there are."

"How many what?"

"Boys . . . outside tonight."

Jamieson, who was weighed down by a far more desperate fear, sighed. "Veda, I've got to go to work tomorrow."

"Work!" said Veda, and her voice had an edge on it. "Don't you even think of anything but work? Haven't you any feelings?"

Jamieson kept his silence, but that was not the way to get her back to bed.

She continued, her voice several tones higher. "The trouble with you men is that you grow callous."

"If you mean by that, am I worried—no, I'm not." That

came hard. He thought, I've got to keep this on this level. He sat up and turned on the light. He said aloud, "Darling, if it gives you any satisfaction, you've succeeded in your purpose. I'm awake."

"It's about time," said Veda. "I think we ought to call up. And if you don't, I will."

Jamieson climbed to his feet. "Okay, but don't you dare hang over my neck when I'm calling. I refuse to have anybody suspect that I'm a hen-pecked husband. You stay right here."

He found himself relieved that she had forced the issue. He went out of the bedroom and shut the door firmly behind him. On the video, he gave his name. There was a pause, and then a grave-faced man in a space admiral's uniform came into view. Jamieson and he were acquainted, officially. His image filled the videoplate as he bent over the videophone in the patrol office.

He said, "Trevor, the situation is as follows: Your son is still in the company of two Rulls—a different pair now, incidentally. They used a very ingenious method to get across the barrier, and at the present moment we suspect that about a hundred Rulls posing as boys are somewhere in The Yards. Nobody has tried to cross in the past half hour, so we feel that every Rull in Solar City who had been prepared against the particular defense we had in the area is now in The Yards. Although they have not yet concentrated on any particular point, we feel that the crisis is imminent."

Jamieson said in a steady tone, "What about my son?"

"Undoubtedly, they have further plans for him. We are trying to provide him with a weapon, but that would have a limited value at best."

Jamieson realized wretchedly that they were being very careful to say nothing that would give him any real hope. He said slowly, "You let a hundred of these

Rulls get into The Way without knowing what they were after?"

The admiral said, "You know how important it is that we learn their objective. What do they value? What do they think is worth such a tremendous risk? This is a very courageous enterprise on their part, and it is our duty to let it come to a head. We are reasonably certain of what they are after, but we must be sure. At the final moment we will make every effort to save your son's life, but we can guarantee nothing."

Jamieson realized clearly how these men regarded the situation. To them, Diddy's death would be a regrettable incident. The papers would say, "Casualties were light." They might even make a hero out of him for a day.

"I'm afraid," said the admiral, "I'll have to ask you to break off now. At this moment your son is going down under the ship, and I want to give my full attention to him. Goodbye."

Jamieson broke the connection and climbed to his feet. He stood for a moment bracing himself, and then he returned to the bedroom and said cheerfully, "Everything seems to be all right."

There was no reply. He saw that Veda was lying with her head on his pillow. She had evidently lain down to await his return and had immediately fallen asleep.

For a woman of her extreme sensitivity, he had done the merciful thing. She slept uneasily, her cheeks wet with tears. He decided to use a gas syringe under pressure to shoot a special sleep-inducing gas into her blood stream. When he did this, there was a pause, and then she relaxed with a drawn-out sigh. Her breathing grew slow and even.

Jamieson phoned Caleb Carson at his apartment and explained the situation. He then added urgently, "Get

Ephraim. Tell him his family needs him; and bring him to Security Headquarters near the ship. Have him well boxed. Don't let anybody see him."

He broke the connection, dressed hurriedly and headed down to the Security Building himself. There would be problems, he knew. There would be resistance on the part of the military brass to the idea of using an ezwal. But the presence of the ezwal was a personal bonus that he and, through him, Diddy had earned.

"What'd that dame whisper to you?" asked Jackie. They were going down the escalator into the tunnel beneath The Way.

Diddy, who had been listening intently for the sound —there wasn't any particular noise—turned. "Oh, just what she said to you."

Jackie seemed to consider that. They reached the walk and Diddy started immediately along it. Casually, he looked for a metal pillar with an H on it. He saw it abruptly, a hundred feet ahead.

Behind him, Gil spoke. "Why would she go to the trouble of whispering to you if she was going to tell us anyway?"

Their suspicion made Diddy tremble inside, but his training won out. "I think she was just having fun with us kids," he said.

"Fun!" That was Jackie.

Gil said, "What are we doing here under the ship?"

Diddy said, "I'm tired." He sat down on the edge of the walk beside the five-foot-thick metal beam that reared up into the distance above. He let his feet dangle down to the tunnel proper. The two Rulls walked past him and stood on the other side of the pillar. Diddy thought with dizzy excitement, They're going to communicate with each other—or with others!

He steadied himself and fumbled under the overlapping edge of the walk with his hand. Swiftly, he ran his fingers under the metal. He touched something. The tiny blaster came easily into his hand, and he slipped it into his pocket in a single synchronized motion. Then, weak from reaction, he sat there. He grew aware of the vibration of the metal on the bones of his thighs. His special shoes had absorbed most of that tremor, and he had been so intent on the weapon that he hadn't noticed immediately. Now he did. Ever so slightly, his body shook and shivered. He felt himself drawn into the sound. His muscles and organs hummed and quivered. Momentarily, he forgot the Rulls, and for that moment it seemed immeasurably strange to be sitting here on the raw metal, unprotected and in tune with the sound itself. He'd guessed the vibration would be terrific under the ship of ships. The city of The Yards was built on metal. But all the shock-absorbing material with which the streets and roads were carpeted couldn't muffle the ultimately violent forces and energies that had been concentrated in one small area. Here were atomic piles so hot that they were exploding continuously with a maximum detonation short of cataclysm. Here were machines that could stamp out hundred-ton electro-steel plates.

For eight and a half years more, The Yards would exist for this colossal ship. And then, when it finally flew, he would be on it. Every family in The Yards had been selected for two purposes—because the father or mother had a skill that could be used in the building of the ship, or because they had a child who would grow up around the ship. His father, being top government personnel, had been included by request.

In no other way, except by growing up with it, would human beings ever learn to understand and operate the spaceship that was rising here like a young mountain. In its ninety-four hundred feet of length was concentrated the engineering genius of centuries, so much specialized knowledge, so much mechanical detail, that visiting dignitaries looked around in bewilderment at the acres of machines and dials and instruments on every floor, and at the flashing wall lights that had already been installed in the lower decks.

He would be on it. Diddy stood up in a shaking excitement of anticipation—just as the two Rulls emerged from behind the pillar.

"Let's go!" said Jackie. "We've fooled around long enough."

Diddy came down from his height of exaltation. "Where to?"

Gil said, "We've been tagging along after you. Now, how about your going where we want to go for a change?"

Diddy did not even think of objecting. "Sure," he said.

The neon sign on the building said, "RESEARCH," and there were a lot of boys around. They wandered singly and in groups. He could see others in the distance, looking as if they were going nowhere in particular. Could any of those others be Rulls? Could they all be? But that was silly; he mustn't let his imagination run away with him.

Research. That was what they were after. Here in this building, human beings had developed the anti-Rull bacteria of the barrier. Just what the Rulls would want to know about that process, he had no idea. Perhaps a single bit of information in connection with it would enable them to destroy source material or an organism, and so nullify the entire defense. The Play Square had intimated that such possibilities existed.

All the doors of "Research" were closed, unlike those in the other buildings they had seen.

Jackie said, "You open up, Diddy."

Obediently, Diddy reached for the door handle. He stopped as two men came along the walk.

One of them hailed him. "Hello there, kid. We keep running into you, don't we?"

Diddy let go of the door and turned to face them. They looked like the two "men" who had originally brought him to the barrier and who had made the bacteria test on him. But that would be merely outward appearance. The only Rulls inside the barrier of all those in Solar City would be individuals who had been immunized against the particular bacteria which he had isolated for them at that one part of the barrier.

It would be a coincidence if both The Yards agent images had belonged to that group. Accordingly, these were probably not the same. Not that it mattered.

The spokesman said, "Glad we bumped into you again. We want to conduct another experiment. Now, look, you go inside there. Research is probably protected in a very special fashion. If we can prove our idea here, then we'll have helped in making it harder for the Rulls to come into The Yards. That'll be worth doing, won't it?"

Diddy nodded. He was feeling kind of sick inside, and he wasn't sure he could talk plainly in spite of all his training.

"Go inside," said the Rull, "stand around for a few moments, and then take a deep breath, hold it in, and come out. That's all."

Diddy opened the door, stepped through into the bright interior. The door closed automatically behind him. He found himself in a large room. I could run, he thought. They don't dare come in here. The absence of people inside the room chilled the impulse. It seemed unusual that there was no one around. Most of the departments in The Yards operated on a round-the-clock basis.

Behind him, the door opened. Diddy turned. The only Rulls in sight were Jackie and Gil standing well back from the door, and other boys even farther away. Whoever had opened the door was taking no chances on getting a dose of anything, dangerous or otherwise.

"You can come out now," said the man's voice. He spoke from behind the door. "But remember, first take a deep breath and hold it."

Diddy took the breath. The door shut automatically as he emerged, and there were the two Yard police waiting behind it. One of them held up a little bottle with a rubber tube. "Exhale into this," he said.

When that was done, the Rull handed it to his companion, who walked quickly around the corner of the building and out of sight.

The spokesman said, "Notice anything unusual?"

Diddy hesitated. The air in the building, now that he thought of it, had seemed thick, a little harder to breathe than ordinary air. He shook his head slowly. "I don't think so," he said.

The Rull was tolerant. "Well, you probably wouldn't notice," he said; then he added quickly, "We might as well test your blood too. Hold up your finger."

Diddy cringed a little from the needle, but he allowed the blood to be taken. Gil came forward. "Can I help?" he asked eagerly.

"Sure," said the man. "You take this around to my friend."

Gil was gone exactly as a boy would go—at a dead run. A minute ticked by, and then another minute; and then . . .

"Ah," said the man, "here they come."

Diddy stared at the returning pair with a sickly grin. The Rull, who had been standing beside him, walked swiftly forward to meet the two. If the two spies said anything to each other, Diddy was unable to hear it.

Actually, he took it for granted that there was a swift exchange on the light level. The communication, whatever its nature, stopped.

The man who had done all the talking came back to Diddy and said, "Kid, you've sure been valuable to us. It looks as if we're really going to make a contribution to the war against the Rulls. Do you know that air in there has an artificial gas mixed with it, a fluorine compound? Very interesting and very safe by itself. And even if a Rull with his fluorine metabolism should walk in there, he'd be perfectly safe—unless he tried to use the energy of his body on a blaster or communication level. The energy would act as an ionizing agent, bring about a molecular union between the fluorine in the air and the fluorine in the Rull body. The union wouldn't last long, being unstable, but neither would the Rull body."

Diddy did not fully understand. The chemical reactions of fluorine and its compounds had been discussed in a general way as part of his teaching, but this was something a little different.

"Very clever," said the spy with apparent satisfaction. "The Rull himself sets off the reaction which destroys him. But now, I gather that all you kids want to go inside and have a look around. Okay, in with you. Not you—" to Diddy—"not for a minute. I want to have a little talk with you. Come on over here."

He drew Diddy aside, while the "boys" rushed through the door. Diddy could imagine them spreading through the building, searching out secrets. He thought wearily, Surely somebody will do something and quickly.

The Rull said, "Confidentially, kid, this is really an important job you've done for us today. Just to give you an idea, we've kept an eye on the Research Building pretty well all night. The staff here usually goes home around midnight. Since midnight a couple of workmen have gone into the place, installed some equipment, and left. They put a radio hook-up over the door, with a loudspeaker both inside and out. If I were a Rull, I'd wreck a thing like that, just as a precaution. Right now, except for you kids, the whole place is empty. You can see how much the people here have depended on the bacteria barrier keeping the Rull away."

He paused, then continued. "Of course the Rulls could spy out most of that information in advance, and if they finally got across the barrier they could set up guards all around the building, and so prevent even the most powerful armored forces from getting through to the defense of the building. It could be blasted, of course, from a distance and destroyed, but it's hard to imagine them doing that very quickly. They'd wait till they'd tried other methods.

"You see where that would take us. The Rulls would have an opportunity to search out some of the secrets of the building. Once outside, they could communicate the information to other Rulls not in the danger area, and then each individual would have to take his own chance on escaping. That's bold stuff, but the Rulls have done similar things before. So you see, it all could happen easily enough. But now we've prevented it."

"Diddy—" it was a whisper from above to one side of him—"don't show any sign that you hear this."

Diddy stiffened, then quickly relaxed. It had been proved long ago that the Rull electronic hearing and talking devices, located as they were inside the sound-deadening shoulder muscles, could not detect whispers.

The whisper continued swiftly. "You've got to go inside. When you are inside, stay near the door. That's all. There'll be more instructions for you then."

Diddy located the source of the whisper. It was coming from above the door. He thought shakily, The Rull mentioned a radio being installed over the door—the whisper must be coming through that.

But how was he going to get inside when this Rull was so obviously delaying him? The Rull was saying something about a reward, but Diddy scarcely heard him. Distractedly, he looked around. He could see a long line of buildings, some of them brightly illuminated, others in half darkness. The vast brilliance from the ship cast a long shadow where he was standing. In the sky above, the night seemed as black as ever.

There was no sign of the bright new morning, only hours away now. Diddy said desperately, "Gosh, I'd better get inside. The sun will soon be up, and I've still got a lot of places to look."

The Rull said, "I wouldn't waste much time in there. But take a look inside anyway. There is something I want you to do."

Quiveringly, Diddy opened the door. The Rull caught it before it could close.

"Let me get in there for just a second," he said.

He stepped in and reached up above the door, and yanked. Some wiring came down.

He stepped back outside. "Just thought I'd create a war condition for our little experiment. I just disconnected the wiring of the newly installed speaker system. You go in for a minute and tell me what the other kids are doing."

The door closed behind Diddy in its automatic fashion.

At the Security Building, the admiral in charge shrugged regretfully at Jamieson. "I'm sorry, Trevor. We did the best we could. But they just wrecked our only hope of contact with your boy."

"What message did you plan to give him?" asked Jamieson.

"I'm sorry," the admiral replied, "that's classified."

From his cage in the trailer outside the building, the ezwal telepathed to Jamieson. "I read his mind. Would you like me to transmit to Diddy?"

"Yes," said Jamieson mentally.

To Diddy, the message that came was clear and direct—and so sharp that he confused it with a whispered speech. The message was: "Diddy, unless a Rull carries a weapon right out in the open, he's dependent on the energy from his cells. A Rull by his very nature has to go about without any clothes on. It's only his body that can produce the images of human clothes and human forms. I see that only two boys are in sight."

There *were* two, boys of whom were bending over a desk on the far side of the room. For a moment Diddy wondered how they were seeing this scene. He had no time for speculation, for the next words came. "Take out your gun and shoot them."

Diddy put his hand in his pocket, swallowed hard and brought out the gun. His hand trembled a little, but for five years now he had been trained for such a moment as this, and he felt awfully steady inside. It was not a gun that had to be aimed perfectly.

He fired a steady blue streak of flame, and he merely waved its nozzle toward where, the Rulls were. They started to run and collapsed as they did so.

"Good shot," said the ezwal.

Diddy scarcely noticed that no sound accompanied the words. Across the room, what had been two applecheeked boys were changing. In death, the images couldn't hold. And though he had seen pictures of what was emerging, it was different seeing the dark flesh coming into view, the strange reticulated limbs.

"Listen—" the thought brought him out of that shock—"all the doors are locked. Nobody can get in. Nobody out. Start walking through the building. Shoot everybody you see. *Everybody!* Accept no pleas, no pretense that they are just kids. Careful track has been kept of every other real boy, and there are only Rulls in the building. Burn them all without mercy."

It was several minutes later that the ezwal reported to Jamieson: "Your son has destroyed every Rull inside the building. I've told him to remain inside, since an attempt is being made to kill those that are outside. He'll stay there until I tell him to come out."

On receiving that message, Jamieson gave a shuddering sigh of relief. "Thank you, my friend," he said silently. "That was an outstanding telepathic performance."

It was the admiral who wanted to talk to Jamieson, later. "It was really a tremendous victory," he said. "The Rulls on the outside fought it out with us in their usual brave fashion, but we changed the bacteria where they originally crossed the barrier, and so we had them trapped."

He hesitated, then said in a puzzled tone, "What I don't understand is, how did your boy know exactly when to use the blaster on them, without our telling him?"

Jamieson said, "I want you to remember that question when you receive my report on what happened."

"Why would you write a report on this incident?" the officer asked, puzzled.

"You'll see," said Jamieson.

It was still pitch-dark as Diddy caught a helicar at Cross 2 and flew to within a block of the hill, from which "Explorers" like himself had to watch the sunrise. He climbed the steps that led to the top of the hill and found several other boys already there, sitting and standing around.

While he could not be certain that they were human, he had a pretty strong conviction that they were. There seemed to be no reason why a Rull should participate in this particular ritual.

Diddy sank down under a bush beside the shadow shape of one of the boys. Neither of them spoke right away; then Diddy said, "What's your name?"

"Mart." The answering voice was shrill but not loud.

"Find the sound?" asked Diddy.

"Yep."

"So did I." He hesitated, thinking of what he had done. Just for a moment he had a sharp awareness of how wonderful was the training that had made it possible for a nine-year-old boy to act as he had acted. Then that faded from his fore-consciousness, and he said, "It's been fun, hasn't it?

"I guess so."

There was silence. From where Diddy sat, he could see the intermittent glare of furnaces as the sky flared with a white, reflected fire. Farther along was the jewel-bright aura of light that partially framed the ship. The sky above was no longer dark, and Diddy noticed that the shadows around him were not dense any more, but grayish. He could see Mart's body crouched under the bush, a smaller body than his own.

As the dawn brightened, he watched the ship. Slowly, the metal of its bare upper ribs caught the flames of the sun that was still not visible from where they sat. The glare expanded downward, and the sunlight glinted on the dark, shiny vastness of its finished lower walls, the solid shape it made against the sky beyond.

Out of the shadows grew the ship, an unbelievable thing, bigger than anything around it. At this distance the hundred-story Administration Building looked like a part of its scaffolding, a white pillar against the dark colossus that was the ship. Long after the sun had come up, Diddy stood watching it in exaltation of pride. In the glare of the new day the ship seemed to be gathering itself as if poised for flight. Not yet, Diddy thought shakily, not yet. But the day would come. In that far time the biggest ship ever planned and constructed by Man would point its nose at the open spaces between the near stars and fly out into the darkness. And then indeed would the Rulls have to give ground.

At last, in response to the familiar empty feeling in his belly, Diddy went down the hill. He ate breakfast in a little "Instant" restaurant. And then, happy, he boarded a helicar and headed for home.

In the master bedroom, Jamieson heard the outer door of the apartment open. He caught his wife with her fingers on the knob of the bedroom door. He shook his head at her gently. "He'll be tired," he said softly. "Let him rest."

Reluctantly, she allowed herself to be led back. To her own bed this time.

Diddy tiptoed across the living room and into the privacy of the Play Square. The door shut automatically behind him as he entered, and the lights switched on. A glance at the controls on the wall showed that the complex robot room was alert to his presence. It said, finally, "Your report, please."

"I found out what the sound was," said Diddy happily.

"What is it?"

When Diddy had answered that, the Play Square said, "You are a credit to my training. I'm proud of you. Now go to sleep."

As he crept under the sheets, Diddy grew aware of the faint tremor of the room. Lying there, he felt the quaver of his bed and heard the shudder of the absorbent plastic windows. Below him the floor creaked ever so faintly in its remote, never ending rapport with the all-pervading vibration.

He grinned happily, but with a great weariness. He'd never have to wonder about the sound again. It was a miasma of The Yards, a thin smoke of vibration from the masses of buildings and metal and machines that tendriled out from The Way.

That sound would be with him all his life; for when the ship was finished, a similar, pervasive sound would shake from every metal plate.

He slept, feeling the pulse of the sound deep inside him, a part of his life.

XX

JAMIESON AWAKENED at his usual hour; and he was in the act of slipping quietly out of bed when he remembered. He turned, looked down at his wife, and shook his head happily. She seemed to be resting well.

She and the boy should sleep for hours still. He turned and tiptoed into his dressing room. He ate breakfast alone and considered how the night's events might affect the long days ahead. That they would affect it, he was convinced.

The ezwal had proved itself. To have done so by saving his son was simply the result of his own determination to use every possible means of helping the boy in his sustained period of danger.

Arrived at his office, Jamieson prepared a report on the night's action. He gave as his final conclusion that what had happened was as important as the completion of the ship itself. He wrote: "The usefulness of mental telepathy as a means of communication with the alien races which now provide so little aid against the common Rull enemy is of course a matter for careful experimentation. But that such a medium of communication exists at all is an outstanding event in the history of the galaxy."

He had the report duplicated, and he sent it by special messenger to everyone he could think of whose opinion would have influence.

The first response came that afternoon from a high Armed Forces figure.

"Were precautions taken to insure that the ezwal did not have mental access to anyone who knew the secrets of Interim Research?" (*Interim* was a code word meaning *Top Secret*.) "Is it possible that this particular ezwal should be destroyed as a matter of simple precaution?"

Jamieson read the message with a feeling that he was dealing with a form of insanity, which of course he was. He had noticed the extremes to which military secrecy was sometimes carried.

He saw that the great man's reply had been sent to all the people to whom he had submitted his own report.

Galvanized, he prepared a reply which established on a basis of data which could be checked that the ezwal had not been near anyone who knew the actual scientific details of Interim Research. He pointed out that though his own knowledge had always been kept at a generalized minimum, the action of the Rull agents, in crossing the barriers, and in their other actions, had indicated a considerable knowledge of the bacterial-warfare methods being used against them; and that rather than condemn the ezwal for the small amount of data which he may have learned from us, we might be well advised to discover what he had learned from the Rull agents.

That was the one distortion in his reply. He knew from

the experience of the giant adult ezwal on Eristan II that ezwals could not read the mind of a Rull. But this was not the moment to present negative information.

He continued. "It is also worth pointing out that it would require months, possibly years, to create again a circumstance whereby a young and willing ezwal falls into our hands. It is also worth pointing out that future relations with the ezwal race will depend on how meticulously we handle ourselves at present. It they should ever become aware that we actually executed a baby ezwal knowing what we now do, the entire relationship would be instantly jeopardized."

Jamieson dispatched his reply, with copies to everyone. And since he still had the ezwal under his care, he took the precaution of having it moved to a new location, for the purpose—he wrote in his report—of making absolutely sure that it had no contact with anyone possessing valuable data.

The report sheet was filed in his own office, for the record.

Satisfied that the ezwal would not now be destroyed by some hasty action taken without his knowledge, he waited for further reactions.

There were several before the end of the afternoon. With one exception, they were acknowledgments only. The exception was from the individual who had responded earlier. It was a personal note to Jamieson, which read: "My God, man, was that monster you showed us a baby?"

That was the last attempt to destroy the young ezwal for legal or military reasons.

A week went by.

Jamieson received a memorandum from Computer Division shortly before noon. "Some data is available on your request of the 10th instant, for names of races with which it has been impossible to establish communication."

He called Caleb Carson, arranged for the two of them to have lunch, with a view of spending part of the afternoon together at Computer Division.

Carson in the flesh was a lean, lantern-jawed individual who bore a strong resemblance to his famous explorer grandfather. There was a glow about him, an air of suppressed excitement, as if he knew secrets and had had experiences which he could not share with anyone.

Seated in the "Ship Room" of the government restaurant for executives, Jamieson told young Carson, "My purpose is to take the ezwal on one journey, to an alien planet, myself. I want to have the experience of using him at least once as a communication medium. Then I'd like to turn him over to you."

Caleb Carson nodded. He looked flushed and eager. He said, "I appreciate this, sir. You're giving me an opportunity to open up entire planets for cooperation with the galactic culture. I haven't operated on that level of things before."

Jamieson nodded but said nothing. He recalled his own feelings years before when he also had been assigned to a level of operations which involved using his own discretion in dealing with entire planets. It was a little startling to realize that he had now reached the stage where he could sign authorization that would give others the same power.

. . . The power to commandeer spaceships.

. . . The power to sign agreements that would bind Earth for a time.

. . . Power . . .

He recalled his own impression of the men who had given him the right to function at such a level of things. He had thought that they were middle-aged. Was he like that? he wondered. He hadn't thought of it more than fleetingly before.

They began to discuss such details as how much freedom the ezwal should have for its own and everyone else's good. They finished lunch. took a last look at the ship—which was towering visibly through the transparent walls; and then, as they walked out, Carson said, "Do they actually plan to go to the Rull home planet with that ship?"

He must have seen, from Jamieson's expression, that he'd said the wrong thing. He sighed. "All right, let's pause at the guardhouse and see if I'm a Rull."

Jamieson nodded grimly. "And while we're about it," he said, "for your sake I'd better be checked also."

They went through the procedure in deadly earnest; were presently cleared, though—Jamieson knew—only for the time being.

In a world of Rull agents, who could mimic human beings, clearance was always a temporary thing. One wrong question, one suspicious action, and the test had to be repeated.

In a sense, a man need merely touch a Rull suspect to establish his humanness. But since few individuals were capable of dealing with a Rull, the prescribed procedure was to report one's suspicions at once to the authorities. The fact that Carson instantly volunteered to be checked almost of itself established that he was human. But the checkup had to be made just the same.

On their way down to Computer Division, Carson said briskly, "For the moment, at least, I can speak freely. On what basis is the Computer selecting alien races?"

Jamieson answered without hesitation. "Sheer alienness plus characteristics that might be useful in the Rull-human war. I'd like to test the ezwal's mental telepathy in extreme circumstances. We've had only one failure so far."

He explained about the inability to contact the Rulls, then went on. "Since there's some possibility that the Rulls are actually from another galaxy, I'm guessing blindly that all life in our Milky Way galaxy is somehow related."

Actually, no one could question such a speculation. Man had discovered myriad facts about life and how it functioned. What life was, or why, was still an unknown that grew more bewildering as the vastness of space was revealed to human beings who manned the far-reaching spaceships and penetrated ever deeper and looked farther into the unfathomable and apparently unending distances of the continuum. In such a universe men could at best make educated guesses. It seemed to Jamieson that he had noticed things about life which justified his own guess.

"Have you any race in mind?" Carson asked.

"No. I fed my requirements into the Computer. I'll let it decide."

They were silent the rest of the way down. A technician led them into a little room, and presently a ticker-tape typewriter began to click loudly. Jamieson looked at the first sentence, whistled softly to himself, and said, "I should have thought of them myself. The Ploians, of course. Who else in all this galaxy?"

"The Ploians!" said Carson, frowning. "Isn't that just a myth? Are we certain there is a Ploian race?"

Jamieson was cheerful. "No, we're not. But it's a perfect time to find out." He was excited. He had forgotten about the Ploians. It would certainly be a severe test for the ezwal, and for his own concept that there was a link between races in the same galaxy.

The specially constructed lifeboat slipped out of the cruiser into space and began to fall toward the planet of Ploia below, on a long, slanting dive. Jamieson kept the power on by remote control, braking the small ship gradually.

He watched the temperature and speed gauges, as the machine entered the tenuous outer reaches of the atmosphere, and continued applying a brake on its speed. As a result, only the outer walls of the lifeboat heated up.

It continued to descend at a normal speed through its electrical and electronic robots. It came down to less than forty miles above the surface of the planet, falling now at about five thousand feet a minute. At twenty miles, Jamieson slowed it even more—until it was drifting along at less than thirty miles an hour. He was in the act of straightening its flight to a horizontal course when the airlock gauge reacted abnormally.

The airlock opened. And shut.

Jamieson waited expectantly.

Abruptly, the needles on his gauges reacted to a surge of power. Instantly, the lifeboat began an erratic and uncontrollable flight. The speed of its fall increased enormously. It twisted to and fro, as if it were out of control.

Jamieson touched one after another of his remote-control devices. The lifeboat continued its unstable flight unchecked. Not one of his electronic robots responded to anything he did during the moments that followed.

Tense but matter-of-fact, Jamieson leaned back to wait. He had expected this to happen. Now that it had there was nothing to do but allow certain conditions to be created by whatever agency had taken over the ship.

The conditions were achieved automatically as the lifeboat reached a level of twenty thousand feet above the green land below.

Aboard it, a machine that was not electrical in nature reacted to a barometer reading. As a result, a weighted wheel moved, and all the electrical power aboard the lifeboat shut off. Other purely mechanical devices were activated by the wind stream of a free fall. The airlock locked mechanically. Rockets boiled into fiery life, and presently the lifeboat, operating on nonelectrical machinery, was climbing back toward space.

Like a bullet in the full fury of its flight, it came shooting up into airless space. Jamieson watched it now through his viewers, with radar. At such distances, it was impossible to determine if whatever had got aboard had managed to resolve the mechanical problem of unlocking the airlock without the use of electric power. He doubted that it had. Accordingly, he had captured a Ploian.

The original Earth expedition had landed on Ploia approximately a hundred years before. Instantly, it found itself in a nightmare. The metal floor, metal furniture and simple metal objects lying around were suddenly conducting electricity as freely as if they were a part of the electrical system of the ship. Scientifically, it was a fantastically interesting phenomenon.

To the eighty-one men who were electrocuted in those first deadly moments, the manifestations were of no further interest whatsoever.

The hundred and forty other crewmen who happened not to be touching metal during those first moments were highly experienced and highly trained. Only twenty-two of them did not realize promptly that they were dealing with electrical phenomena. The twenty-two were later buried, along with the first unlucky group, in a land that was as green and virgin as the most primitive planet ever discovered by man.

The survivors tried first of all to take back control of their ship. They shut off all power. Reasoning that some kind of life organism had gotten aboard, they began a systematic housecleaning, using chemical sprays. When the entire ship was saturated, they turned on the power.

After a moment, it went as wild as before. They tried all their chemical sprays in turn, without result. Boldly, they went outside, connected a hose to water, and set off the ship's sprinkler system. Every cubic inch of space inside was subjected to a pressurized stream.

That, also, had no effect. Indeed, whatever had come aboard was so sentient that it had observed how they started and stopped the dynamos. During one of the sleep watches, while half the men dozed uneasily, all the electrical machines started simultaneously. They had to cut connections, with power tools, before that was brought under control.

Meanwhile, mirrors were used to contact a companion cruiser which "floated" in an orbit above the atmosphere. The half-mad terrified crew below was given an analysis of their situation which confirmed their own observations.

"The aliens," they were advised, "do not seem to be directly inimical to human beings. All deaths appear to be accidental results of their interference with the electrical system of the ship. It may therefore be postulated that a study can be made of this life form, by setting up various combinations of electrical phenomena and watching the reaction. Instruments for this purpose will be devised and will be dropped to you."

The expedition became scientific. And for six months the phenomena of a strange life form were studied. The end result was not satisfactory, because at no time was contact established, nor was it finally determined that a life form actually existed on the planet.

At the end of the half year, the companion cruiser dropped several old-style rockets, which utilized non-electrical firing mechanisms. And so the survivors of the first expedition to Ploia were rescued.

Jamieson thought of all this as he used tractor beams to draw his lifeboat into an airlock of his own cruiser.

A few moments later the great ship was speeding out into interstellar space.

There was nothing decisive to do immediately. The ezwal reported the presence of another "mind" but could not pin down any thought other than anxiety and unhappiness.

The indication that there was *something* eased Jamieson's own mind considerably. In view of the experience of the first expedition, he had not been able to escape the feeling that he was deluding himself. By identifying a presence, the ezwal was already serving a useful purpose.

A hundred light-years from Ploia, he disconnected the interstellar drives from all electrical connections. Then he and the ezwal retreated into a part of the ship specially constructed for this journey. It was connected to the main section by motor-driven and hand-operated mechanisms. In it was a second control board. From it, using a specially built mechanical device, Jamieson opened the airlock of the lifeboat and allowed the Ploian to enter the main part of the ship—if that strange being chose to do so.

The ezwal reported in his swift mental fashion. "I have pictures of scenes in the main control room. They seem to come from near the ceiling. I have the impression he is sizing up the situation."

That seemed reasonably decisive. The Ploian's mind could be read. Jamieson could imagine himself in a similar predicament aboard an alien ship. He guessed how wary he would be.

"Now he's gone into the control board," flashed the ezwal.

"*Into it?*" Jamieson asked, startled.

There was a jerk, and the ship darted off at an angle from its course. The erratic course did not disturb Jamieson. But his new knowledge of the Ploian—

179

gained from the ezwal—made a startling picture of a short-circuited control board. He visualized an amorphous creature creeping and slithering through a mass of wires and instruments, its "body" a bridge for the live power in the numerous relays.

Even as he had the picture, the ship's course steadied. The great vessel plunged in a line drive through that remote edge of the galaxy.

The ezwal's thought came. "He selected a direction and has a plan to go in that direction exactly as long as we did, earlier. He knows nothing of faster drives."

Jamieson shook his head, impressed but pitying. Poor Ploian! Caught in a trap of distance the like of which his race had never seen or even, perhaps, guessed.

Aloud, he said, presently, "Tell him how great the distance is. Tell him about the difference between the interstellar drive and the drive he's using."

The ezwal said, "I've told him. All I got back is rage."

"Keep telling him," said Jamieson steadily.

Later he said, "Tell him that we have an electrically operated machine through which he and I can talk to each other—once he learns its mechanism."

Still later, Jamieson instructed, "Ask him what he uses for food."

And that brought the first reply.

"He says," reported the ezwal, "that he's dying, and that we're responsible."

It was telepathy in full. Presently, they had the information that Ploians lived off the magnetic force of their planet, which they converted into a sort of life energy.

With the electrical system dead, no magnetic flux was available from the numerous coils and armatures of electric motors, generators, relays and magnetrons. Ephraim received the impression that such concentrations of flux were extremely exhilarating to Ploians.

It occurred to Jamieson that this simple reaction would

account for much if not all the damage the Ploians had inflicted on the previous explorers. He had a sudden visualization that all the wreckage of equipment, and the deadly effect on the human crew, had largely been incidental to a sort of "jag" enjoyed by the Ploians.

With that in mind, it was no trick to set up a small gas turbine to drive a generator, which, in turn, operated the electric motor of a compressor.

"Tell him," said Jamieson to the ezwal, "not to assimilate the flux too fast, or he'll stall the system."

They gave the Ploian his "meal." Then: "Now tell him said Jamieson, "no more nourishment until he agrees to work that communication machine."

Within hours, the Ploian could so modulate electrical current that intelligible if rather gutteral speech sounds came over the speaker of the voice machine. The being acquired an acceptable command of English in one day.

"The question is," said Jamieson, more to himself than to the young ezwal, "what kind of IQ does this fellow have, to learn a language as rapidly as that?"

Ephraim could not comment on that directly, having no need for language. But he did report: "He seems to have his entire energy field available for storing memories, and that field extends out almost as far as he wants it to."

Jamieson considered that, but he was unable to obtain a clear mental picture of such a "nervous system." He said finally, "On our way home, I'm going to put together a miniature version of that communication machine, so I can wear it in my ear. I'd like to train him to the point where I can talk to him as easily as I do to you."

He manufactured the instrument and was in process of giving the training when two messages arrived for him from Earth. They changed his plans for the immediate future.

The first message was from Caleb Carson: "Political switch on Carson's Planet makes possible educational program for ezwals without waiting for Galactic Convention. A Mrs. Whitman is the source of this information. She said you would understand."

Jamieson's comment on that message was wry: "There was a time when Mrs. Whitman and I didn't like each other. I presume that has now changed. I guess I'm willing."

The second message was equally decisive: "Proceed at once to newly discovered planet in Region 18. Location will be scrambled on 1–8–3–18–26–54–6. You are commanded to make personal survey and report asap. Signed, SUCOMSPAOP."

Jamieson did not need to be told why the Supreme Commander of Space Operations had concerned himself directly. Region 18 was code for the farthest forward "line" of the anti-Rull forces. Along with Carson's Planet, and two others, this new world would make up a foursome of military bastions from which Earth—and man's part of the galaxy—could be defended.

The numbers simply indicated the code by which the location of the new planet would be radioed to him.

On receipt of the messages, Jamieson altered his plans.

He acknowledged both messages immediately. To Caleb Carson he radioed: "Meet me at——" He named a planet which he and Carson could both reach at approximately the same time. "Will turn Ephraim and this ship over to you and you proceed to Carson's Planet and carry on as planned."

To SUCOMSPAOP he radioed: "Have warship meet me at——" He named the planet where he would meet Caleb

Carson. "And be prepared to take aboard my personal lifeboat."

It was the only good solution to the problem presented by the Ploian—take him along.

Earnestly, Jamieson impressed upon that being the importance of not doing anything rash. "If you ever hope to get back to your own planet, you'll have to do exactly as I say at all times," he said.

The Ploian promised faithfully and soberly.

XXI

TREVOR JAMIESON saw the other space boat out of the corner of his eye. He was sitting in a hollow about a dozen yards from the edge of the precipice, and some score of feet from the doorway of his own lifeboat. He had been intent on his survey book, annotating a comment beside the voice graph, to the effect that Laertes III was so close to the invisible dividing line between Earth-controlled and Rull-controlled space that its prior discovery by man was in itself a major victory in the Rull-human war.

He had written: "The fact that ships based on this planet could strike at several of the most densely populated areas of the galaxy, *Rull or human,* gives it an AA priority on all available military equipment. Preliminary defense units should be set up on Mount Monolith, where I am now, within three weeks. . . ."

It was at that point that he saw the other boat, above

and somewhat to his left, approaching the tableland. He glanced up at it, and froze where he was, torn between two opposing purposes. His first impulse, to run for the lifeboat, yielded to the realization that the movement would be seen instantly by the electronic reflexes of the other ship. For a moment, then, he had the dim hope that, if he remained quiet enough, neither he nor his ship would be observed.

Even as he sat there, perspiring with indecision, his tensed eyes noted the Rull markings and the rakish design of the other vessel. His vast knowledge of things Rull enabled him to catalogue it instantly as a survey craft.

A *survey* craft. The Rulls had discovered the Laertes sun.

The terrible potentiality was that, behind this small craft, might be fleets of battleships, whereas he was alone. His own lifeboat had been dropped by the *Orion* nearly a parsec away, while the big ship was proceeding at antigravity speeds. That was to insure that Rull energy tracers did not record its passage through this area of space. The *Orion* was to head for the nearest base, load up with planetary defense equipment, and then return. She was due in ten days.

Ten days. Jamieson groaned inwardly and drew his legs under him and clenched his hand about the survey book. But still the possibility that his ship, partially hidden under a clump of trees, might escape notice if *he* remained quiet, held him there in the open. His head tilted up, his eyes glared at the alien, and his brain willed it to turn aside. Once more, while he waited, the implications of the disaster that could be here struck deep.

The Rull ship was a hundred yards away now and showed no signs of changing its course. In seconds it would cross the clump of trees, which half hid the lifeboat.

In a spasm of movement, Jamieson launched himself from his chair. With complete abandon, he dived for the open doorway of his machine. As the door clanged behind him, the boat shook as if it had been struck by a giant. Part of the ceiling sagged; the floor heaved under him, and the air grew hot and suffocating. Gasping, Jamieson slid into the control chair and struck the main emergency switch. The rapid-fire blasters huzzaed into automatic firing positions and let go with a hum and a deep-throated *ping*. The refrigerators whined with power; a cold blast of air blew at his body. The relief was so quick that a second passed before Jamieson realized that the atomic engines had failed to respond. And that the lifeboat, which should have already been sliding into the air, was still lying inert in an exposed position.

Tense, he stared into the visiplates. It took a moment to locate the Rull ship. It was at the lower edge of one plate, tumbling slowly out of sight beyond a clump of trees a quarter of a mile away. As he watched, it disappeared; and then the crash of the landing came clear and unmistakable from the sound board in front of him.

The relief that came was weighted with an awful reaction. Jamieson sank into the cushions of the control chair, weak from the narrowness of his escape. The weakness ended abruptly as a thought struck him. There had been a sedateness about the way the enemy ship fell. *The crash hadn't killed the Rulls aboard.* He was alone in a damaged lifeboat on an impassable mountain with one or more of the most remorseless creatures ever spawned. For ten days he must fight in the hope that man would still be able to seize the most valuable planet discovered in half a century.

Jamieson opened the door and went out onto the tableland. He was still trembling with reaction, but it was rapidly growing darker and there was no time to waste. He walked quickly to the top of the nearest hillock a hundred feet away, taking the last few feet on his hands and knees. Cautiously, he peered over the rim. Most of the mountaintop was visible. It was a rough oval some eight hundred yards wide at its narrowest, a wilderness of scraggly brush and upjutting rock, dominated here and there by clumps of trees. There was not a movement to be seen, and not a sign of the Rull ship. Over everything lay an atmosphere of desolation, and the utter silence of an uninhabited wasteland.

The twilight was deeper now that the sun had sunk below the southwest precipice. And the deadly part was that, to the Rulls, with their wider vision and more complete sensory equipment, the darkness would mean nothing. All night long he would have to be on the defensive against beings whose nervous systems outmatched his in every function except, possibly, intelligence. On that level, and that alone, human beings claimed equality. The very comparison made him realize how desperate his situation was. He needed an advantage. If he could get to the Rull wreck and cause them some kind of damage before it got pitch-dark, before they recovered from the shock of the crash, that alone might make the difference between life and death for him.

It was a chance he had to take. Hurriedly, Jamieson backed down the hillock and, climbing to his feet, started along a shallow wash. The ground was rough with stone and projecting edges of rock and the gnarled roots and tangle of hardy growth. Twice he fell, the first time gashing his right hand. It slowed him mentally and physically. He had never before tried to make speed over the pathless wilderness of the tableland. He saw that in ten minutes he had covered a distance of no more than a few hundred yards. He stopped. It was one thing to be bold on the chance of making a vital gain.

It was quite another to throw away his life on a reckless gamble. The defeat would not be his alone but man's.

As he stood there he grew aware of how icy cold it had become. A chilling wind from the east had sprung up. By midnight the temperature would be zero. He began to retreat. There were several defenses to rig up before night; and he had better hurry. An hour later, when the moonless darkness lay heavily over the mountain of mountains, Jamieson sat tensely before his visiplates. It was going to be a long night for a man who dared not sleep. Somewhere about the middle of it, Jamieson saw a movement at the remote perimeter of his all-wave vision plate. Finger on blaster control, he waited for the object to come into sharper focus. It never did. The cold dawn found him weary but still alertly watching for an enemy that was acting as cautiously as he himself. He began to wonder if he had actually seen anything.

Jamieson took another antisleep pill and made a more definite examination of the atomic motors. It didn't take long to verify his earlier diagnosis. The basic gravitation pile had been thoroughly frustrated. Until it could be reactivated on the *Orion*, the motors were useless. The conclusive examination braced him. He was committed irrevocably to this deadly battle of the tableland. The idea that had been turning over in his mind during the night took on new meaning. This was the first time in his knowledge that a Rull and a human being had faced each other on a limited field of action, where neither was a prisoner. The great battles in space were ship against ship and fleet against fleet. Survivors either escaped or were picked up by overwhelming forces.

Unless he was bested before he could get organized, here was a priceless opportunity to try some tests on the Rulls—and without delay. Every moment of daylight must be utilized to the uttermost limit.

Jamieson put on his special "defensive" belts and went outside. The dawn was brightening minute by minute; and the vistas that revealed themselves with each increment of light power held him, even as he tensed his body for the fight ahead. Why, he thought, in a sharp, excited wonder, this is happening on the strangest mountain ever known.

Mount Monolith stood on a level plain and reared up precipitously to a height of eight thousand two hundred feet. The most majestic pillar in the known universe, it easily qualified as one of the hundred natural wonders of the galaxy.

He had walked the soil of planets a hundred thousand light-years from Earth, and the decks of great ships that flashed from the eternal night into the blazing brightness of suns red and suns blue, suns yellow and white and orange and violet, suns so wonderful and different that no previous imaginings could match the reality.

Yet, here he stood on a mountain on far Laertes, one man compelled by circumstances to pit his cunning against one or more of the supremely intelligent Rull enemy.

Jamieson shook himself grimly. It was time to launch his attack—and discover the opposition that could be mustered against him. That was step one, and the important point about it was to insure that it wasn't also step last. By the time the Laertes sun peered palely over the horizon that was the northeast cliff's edge, the assault was under way. The automatic defensors, which he had set up the night before, moved slowly from point to point ahead of the mobile blaster. He cautiously saw to it that one of the three defensors also brought up his rear. He augmented that basic protection by crawling from one projecting rock after another. The machines, he manipulated from a tiny hand control, which was connected to the visiplates that poked out from his headgear just above his eyes. With tensed eyes, he watched the wavering needles that would indicate movement or that the defensor screens were being subjected to energy opposition.

Nothing happened. As he came within sight of the Rull craft, Jamieson halted, while he seriously pondered the problem of no resistance. He didn't like it. It was possible that all the Rulls aboard had been killed, but he doubted it.

Bleakly he studied the wreck through the telescopic eyes of one of the defensors. It lay in a shallow indentation, its nose buried in a wall of gravel. Its lower plates were collapsed versions of the original. His single energy blast of the day before, completely automatic though it had been, had really dealt a smashing blow to the Rull ship.

The over-all effect was of lifelessness. If it were a trick, then it was a very skillful one. Fortunately, there were tests he could make, not final but evidential and indicative.

The echoless height of the most unique mountain ever discovered hummed with the fire sound of the mobile blaster. The noise grew to a roar as the unit's pile warmed to its task and developed its maximum kilocurie of activity. Under that barrage, the hull of the enemy craft trembled a little and changed color slightly, but that was all. After ten minutes, Jamieson cut the power and sat baffled and indecisive.

The defensive screens of the Rull ship were full on. Had they gone on automatically after his first shot of the evening before? Or had they been put up deliberately to nullify just such an attack as this? He couldn't be sure. That was the trouble; he had no positive knowledge.

The Rull could be lying inside dead. (Odd, how he was beginning to think in terms of one rather than several, but the degree of caution being used by the opposition—if opposition existed—matched his own, and indicated the caution of an individual moving against unknown odds.) It could be wounded and incapable of doing anything against him. It could have spent the night marking up the tableland with nerve control lines —he'd have to make sure he never looked directly at the ground—or it could simply be waiting for the arrival of the greater ship that had dropped it onto the planet.

Jamieson refused to consider that last possibility. That way was death, without qualification of hope. Frowning, he studied the visible damage he had done to the ship. All the hard metals had held together, so far as he could see, but the whole bottom of the ship was dented to a depth that varied from one to four feet. Some radiation must have got in, and the question was, what would it have damaged? He had examined dozens of captured Rull survey craft, and if this one ran to the pattern, then in the front would be the control center, with a sealed-aff blaster chamber. In the rear the engine room, two storerooms, one for fuel and equipment, the other for food and—

For food. Jamieson jumped, and then with wide eyes noted how the food section had suffered greater damage than any other part of the ship. Surely, surely, some radiation must have got into it, poisoning it, ruining it, and instantly putting the Rull, with his swift digestive system, into a deadly position.

Jamieson sighed with the intensity of his hope and prepared to retreat. As he turned away, quite incidentally, accidentally, he glanced at the rock behind which he had shielded himself from possible direct fire. Glanced at it and saw the lines on it. Intricate lines, based on a profound and inhuman study of human neurons. He recognized them for what they were and stiffened in horror. He thought, Where—*where* am I being directed?

That much had been discovered after his return from Mira 23, with his report of how he had been apparently, instantly, hypnotized; the lines impelled movement to somewhere. Here, on this fantastic mountain, it could only be to a cliff. But which one?

With a desperate will, he fought to retain his senses a moment longer. He strove to see the lines again. He saw, briefly, flashingly, five wavering verticals and above them three lines that pointed east with their wavering ends. The pressure built up inside him, but still he fought to keep his thoughts self-motivated. Fought to remember if there were any wide ledges near the top of the east cliff. There were. He recalled them in a final agony of hope. There, he thought, that one, that one. Let me fall on that one. He strained to hold the ledge image he wanted and to repeat, many times, the command that might save his life. His last dreary thought was that here was the answer to his doubts. The Rull *was* alive. Blackness came like a curtain of pure essence of night.

XXII

FROM THE FAR GALAXY had he come, a cold, remorseless leader of leaders, the *yeli*, Meesh, the Iin of Ria, the high Aaish of Yeel. And other titles, and other positions, and power. Oh, the power that he had, the power of death, the power of life and the power of the Leard ships.

He had come in his great anger to discover what was wrong. Many years before, the command had been given: Expand into the Second Galaxy. Why were they-who-could-not-be-more-perfect so slow in carrying out these instructions? What was the nature of the two-legged creatures whose multitudinous ships, impregnable planetary bases and numerous allies had fought those-who-possessed-Nature's-supreme-nervous-system to an impasse?

"Bring me a live human being!"

The command echoed to the ends of Riatic space. It produced a dull survivor of an Earth cruiser, a sailor of low degree with an IQ of ninety-six, and a fear index of two hundred and seven. The creature made vague efforts to kill himself, and squirmed on the laboratory tables, and finally escaped into death when the scientists were still in the beginning of the experiments which *he* had ordered to be performed before his own eyes.

"Surely this is not the enemy."

"Sire, we capture so few that are alive. Just as we have conditioned our own, so do they seem to be conditioned to kill themselves in case of capture."

"The environment is wrong. We must create a situation where the captured does not know himself to be a prisoner. Are there any possibilities?"

"The problem will be investigated."

He had come, as the one who would conduct the experiment, to the sun where a man had been observed seven periods before. The man was in a small craft—as the report put it—"which was precipitated suddenly out of subspace and fell toward this sun. The fact that it used no energy aroused the suspicions of our observing warship, which might otherwise have paid no attention to so small a machine. And so, because an investigation was made immediately, we have a new base possibility, and of course an ideal situation for the experiment."

The report continued: "No landings have been made yet, as you instructed; so far as we know, our presence is not suspected. It may be assumed that there was an earlier human landing on the third planet, for the man quickly made that curious mountaintop his headquarters. It will be ideal for your purposes."

A battle group patrolled the space around the sun. But *he* came down in a small ship, and because he had contempt for his enemy, he had flown in over the mountains, fired his disabling blast at the ship on the ground—and then was struck by a surprisingly potent return blast that sent his machine spinning to a crash. Death almost came in those seconds. But he crawled out of his control chair, shocked but still alive. With thoughtful eyes, he assessed the extent of the disaster that had befallen him. He had issued commands that he would call when he wanted them to return. But he could not call. The radio was shattered beyond repair. He had an uneasy sensation when he discovered that his food was poisoned.

Swiftly, he stiffened to the necessity of the situation. The experiment would go on, with one proviso. When the need for food became imperative, he would kill the man, and so survive until the commanders of the ships grew alarmed and came down to see what had happened.

He spent part of the sunless period exploring the cliff's edge. Then he hovered on the perimeter of the man's defensor energies, studying the lifeboat and pondering the possible actions the other might take against him. Finally, with a tireless patience, he examined the approaches to his own ship. At key points, he drew the lines-that-could-seize-the-minds-of-men. There was satisfaction, shortly after the sun came up, in seeing the enemy "caught" and "compelled." The satisfaction had but one drawback. He could not take the advantage of the situation that he wanted. The difficulty was that the man's blaster had been left focused on his main airlock. It was not emitting energy, but the Rull did not doubt that it would fire automatically if the door opened.

What made the situation serious was that, when he tried the emergency exit, it was jammed. It hadn't been. With the forethought of his kind, he had tested it immediately after the crash. Then, it opened. Now it didn't. The ship, he decided, must have settled while he was out during the sunless period. Actually, the reason for what had happened didn't matter. What counted was that he was locked in just when he wanted to be outside. It was not as if he had definitely decided to destroy the man immediately. If capturing him meant gaining control of his food supply, then it would be unnecessary to give him death. It was important to be able to make the decision, however, while the man was helpless. And the further possibility that the *elled* fall might kill him made the *yeli* grim. He didn't like accidents to disturb his plans.

From the beginning the affair had taken a sinister turn. He had been caught up by forces beyond his control, by elements of space and time which he had always taken into account as being theoretically possible, but he had never considered them as having personal application.

That was for the deeps of space where the Leard ships fought to extend the frontiers of the perfect ones. Out there lived alien creatures that had been spawned by Nature before the ultimate nervous system was achieved. All those aliens must die because they were now unnecessary, and because, existing, they might accidentally discover means of upsetting the balance of Yeellian life. In civilized Ria accidents were forbidden.

The Rull drew his mind clear of such weakening thoughts. He decided against trying to open the emergency door. Instead, he turned his blaster against a crack in the hard floor. The frustrators blew their gases across the area where he had worked, and the suction pumps caught the swirling radioactive stuff and drew it into a special chamber. But the lack of an open door as a safety valve made the work dangerous. Many times he paused while the air was cleansed, so that he could come out again from the frustrating chamber to which he retreated whenever the heat made his nerves tingle —a more reliable guide than any instrument that had to be watched.

The sun was past the meridian when the metal plate finally lifted clear and gave him an opening into the gravel and rock underneath. The problem of tunneling out into the open was easy except that it took time and physical effort. Dusty and angry and hungry, the Rull emerged from the hole near the center of the clump of trees beside which his craft had fallen.

His plan to conduct an experiment had lost its attraction. He had obstinate qualities in his nature, but he reasoned that this situation could be reproduced for him on a more civilized level. No need to take risks or to be uncomfortable. He would kill the man and chemically convert him to food until the ships came down to rescue him. With hungry gaze, he searched the ragged, uneven east cliff, peering down at the ledges, crawling swiftly along until he had virtually circumvented the tableland. He found nothing he could be sure about. In one or two places the ground looked lacerated as by the passage of a body, but the most intensive examination failed to establish that anyone had actually been there.

Somberly, the Rull glided toward the man's lifeboat. From a safe distance, he examined it. The defense screens were up, but he couldn't be sure they had been put up before the attack of the morning, or had been raised since then, or had come on automatically at his approach. He couldn't be sure. That was the trouble. Everywhere on the tableland around him was a barrenness, a desolation unlike anything he had ever known. The man could be dead, his smashed body lying at the remote bottom of the mountain. He could be inside the ship badly injured; he had, unfortunately, *had* time to get back to the safety of his craft. Or he could be waiting inside, alert, aggressive, and conscious of his enemy's uncertainty, determined to take full advantage of that uncertainty.

The Rull set up a watching device that would apprise him when the door opened. Then he returned to the tunnel that led into his ship, laboriously crawled through it, and settled himself to wait out the emergency. The hunger in him was an expanding force, hourly taking on a greater urgency. It was time to stop moving around. He would need all his energy for the crisis. The days passed.

Jamieson stirred in an effluvium of pain. At first it seemed all-enveloping, a mist of anguish that bathed him in sweat from head to toe. Gradually, then, it localized in the region of his lower left leg. The pulse of the pain made a rhythm in his nerves. The minutes lengthened into an hour, and then he finally thought, Why, I've got a sprained ankle! There was more to it than that, of course. The pressure that had driven him here oppressed his life force. How long he lay there, partly conscious, was not clear, but when he finally opened his eyes, the sun was still shining on him, though it was almost directly overhead.

He watched it with the mindlessness of a dreamer as it withdrew slowly past the edge of the overhanging precipice. It was not until the shadow of the cliff suddenly plopped across his face that he started to full consciousness with a sudden memory of deadly danger. It took a while for him to shake the remnants of the effect of the nerve lines from his brain. And, even as it was fading, he sized up, to some extent, the difficulties of his position. He saw that he had tumbled over the edge of a cliff to a steep slope. The angle of descent of the slope was a sharp fifty-five degrees, and what had saved him was that his body had been caught in the tangled growth near the edge of the greater precipice beyond. His foot must have twisted in those roots and been sprained.

As he finally realized the nature of his injuries, Jamieson braced up. He was safe. In spite of having suffered an accidental defeat of major proportions, his intense concentration on this slope, his desperate will to make *this* the place where he must fall, had worked out. He began to climb. It was easy enough on the slope, steep as it was; the ground was rough, rocky and scraggly with brush. It was when he came to the ten-foot overhanging cliff that his ankle proved what an obstacle it could be. Four times he slid back reluctantly; and then, on the fifth try, his fingers, groping, caught an unbreakable root. Triumphantly, he dragged himself to the safety of the tableland.

Now that the sound of his scraping and struggling was gone, only his heavy breathing broke the silence of the emptiness. His anxious eyes studied the uneven terrain. The tableland spread before him with not a sign of a moving figure anywhere. To one side, he could see his lifeboat. Jamieson began to crawl toward it, taking care to stay on rock as much as possible. What had happened to the Rull he did not know. And since, for several days, his ankle would keep him inside his ship, he might as well keep his enemy guessing during that time.

It was getting dark, and he was inside the ship, when a peevish voice said in his ear, "When do we go home? When do I eat again?"

It was the Ploian, with his perennial question about returning to Ploia. Jamieson shrugged aside his momentary feeling of guilt. He had forgotten all about his companion these many hours.

As he "fed" the being, he thought, not for the first time, How could he explain the Rull-human war to this untutored mind? More important, how could he explain his present predicament?

Aloud, he said, "Don't you worry. You stay with me, and I'll see that you get home." That—plus the food— seemed to satisfy the being.

For a time, then, Jamieson considered how he might use the Ploian against the Rull. But the fact was that his principal ability was not needed. There was no point in letting a starving Rull discover that his human opponent had a method of scrambling the electrical system of his ship.

XXIII

JAMIESON LAY in his bunk thinking. He could hear the beating of his heart. There were the occasional sounds when he dragged himself out of bed. The radio, when he turned it on, was dead—no static, not even the fading in and out of a wave. At this colossal distance, even subspace radio was impossible. He listened on all the more active Rull wave lengths. But the silence was there too. Not that they would be broadcasting if they were in the vicinity. He was cut off here in this tiny ship on an uninhabited planet with useless motors. He tried not to think of it like that. Here, he told himself, is the opportunity of a lifetime for an experiment. He warmed to the idea as a moth to flame. Live Rulls were hard to get hold of. And here was an ideal situation. *We're prisoners, both of us.* That was the way he tried to picture it. Prisoners of an environment and, therefore, in a curious fashion, prisoners of each other. Only each was free of the conditioned need to kill himself.

There were things a man might discover. The great mysteries—as far as men were concerned—that motivated Rull actions. Why did they want to destroy other races totally? Why did they needlessly sacrifice valuable ships in attacking Earth machines that ventured into their sectors of space when they knew that the intruders would leave in a few weeks anyway?

The potentialities of this fight of man against Rull on a lonely mountain exhilarated Jamieson as he lay on his bunk, scheming, turning the problem over in his mind. There were times during those dog days when he crawled over to the control chair and peered for an hour at a stretch into the visiplates. He saw the tableland and the vista of distance beyond it. He saw the sky of Laertes III, pale orchid in color, silent and lifeless. He saw the prison. Caught here, he thought bleakly. Trevor Jamieson, whose quiet voice in the scientific council chambers of Earth's galactic empire spoke with considerable authority—that Jamieson was here, alone, lying in a bunk, waiting for a leg to heal, so that he might conduct an experiment with a Rull. It seemed incredible. But he grew to believe it as the days passed.

On the third day, he was able to move around sufficiently to handle a few heavy objects. He began work immediately on the light-screen. On the fifth day it was finished. Then the story had to be recorded. That was easy. Each sequence had been so carefully worked out in bed that it flowed from his mind onto the visiwire.

He set it up about two hundred yards from the lifeboat, behind a screening of trees. He tossed a can of food a dozen feet to one side of the screen.

The rest of the day dragged. It was the sixth day since the arrival of the Rull, the fifth since he had sprained his ankle. Came the night.

XXIV

A GLIDING SHADOW, undulating under the starlight of Laertes III, the Rull approached the screen the man had set up. How bright it was, shining in the darkness of the tableland, a blob of light in a black universe of uneven ground and dwarf shrubbery. When he was a hundred feet from the light, he sensed the food—and realized that here was a trap. For the Rull, six days without food had meant a stupendous loss of energy, visual blackouts on a dozen color levels, a dimness of life-force that fitted with the shadows, not the sun. That inner world of disjointed nervous sytem was like a rundown battery, with a score of organic "instruments" disconnecting one by one as the energy level fell. The *yeli* recognized dimly, but with a savage anxiety, that the keenest edges of that nervous system might never be fully restored. Speed was essential. A few more steps downward, and then the old, old conditioning of mandatory self-inflicted death would apply even to the high Aaish of the Yeell.

The reticulated body grew quiet. The visual centers which were everywhere accepted light on a narrow band from the screen. From beginning to end, he watched the story as it unfolded, and then watched it again, craving repetition with all the ardor of a primitive.

The picture began in deep space with the man's lifeboat being dropped from a launching lock of a battleship. It showed the battleship going to a military base, and there taking on supplies and acquiring a vast fleet of reinforcements, and then starting on the return journey. The scene switched to the lifeboat dropping down on Laertes III, showed everything that had subsequently happened, suggested the situation was dangerous to them both—and pointed out the only safe solution. The final sequence of each showing of the story was of the Rull approaching the can, to the left of the screen, and opening it. The method was shown in detail, as was the visualization of the Rull busily eating the food inside. Each time that sequence drew near, a tenseness came over the Rull, a will to make the story real. But it was not until the seventh showing had run its course that he glided forward, closing the last gap between himself and the can. It was a trap, he knew, perhaps even death—it didn't matter. To live, he had to take the chance. Only by this means, by risking what was in the can, could he hope to remain alive for the necessary time.

How long it would take for the commanders cruising

up there in the black of space—how long it would be before they would decide to supersede his command, he didn't know. But they would come. Even if they waited until the enemy ships arrived before they would come. At that point they could come down without fear of suffering from his ire. Until then he would need all the food he could get. Gingerly, he extended a sucker and activated the automatic opener of the can.

It was shortly after four in the morning when Jamieson awakened to the sound of an alarm ringing softly. It was still pitch-dark outside—the Laertes day was twenty-six sidereal hours long, and dawn was still three hours away. He did not get up at once. The alarm had been activated by the opening of the can of food. It continued to ring for a full fifteen minutes, which was just about perfect. The alarm was tuned to the electronic pattern emitted by the can, once it was opened, and so long as any food remained in it. The lapse of time involved fitted with the capacity of one of the Rull mouths in absorbing three pounds of treated food. For fifteen minutes, accordingly, a member of the Rull race, man's mortal enemy, had been subjected to a pattern of mental vibrations corresponding to its own thoughts. It was a pattern to which the nervous systems of other Rulls had responded in laboratory experiments. Unfortunately, those others had killed themselves on awakening, and so no definite results had been proved. But it had been established by the ecphoriometer that the unconscious and not the conscious mind was affected. It was the beginning of hypnotic indoctrination and control.

Jamieson lay in bed, smiling quietly to himself. He turned over finally to go back to sleep, and then he realized how excited he was. It was the greatest moment in the history of Rull-human warfare. Surely he wasn't going to let it pass unremarked. He climbed out of bed and poured himself a drink.

The attempt of the Rull to attack him through his unconscious mind had emphasized his own possible actions in that direction. Each race had discovered some of the weaknesses of the other. Rulls used their knowledge to exterminate. Man tried for communication and hoped for association. Both were ruthless, murderous, pitiless in their methods. Outsiders sometimes had difficulty distinguishing one from the other. But the difference in purpose was as great as the difference between black and white, the absence, as compared to the presence, of light. There was only one trouble with the immediate situation. Now that the Rull had food, he might develop a few plans of his own.

Jamieson returned to bed and lay staring into the darkness. He did not underrate the resources of the Rull, but since he had decided to conduct an experiment, no chances must be considered too great. He turned over finally and slept the sleep of a man determined that things were working in his favor.

Morning. Jamieson put on his cold-proof clothes and went out into the chilly dawn. Again he savored the silence and the atmosphere of isolated grandeur. A strong wind was blowing from the east, and there was an iciness in it that stung his face. He forgot that. There were things to do on this morning of mornings. He would do them with his usual caution.

Paced by defensors and the mobile blaster, he headed for the mental screen. It stood in open high ground, where it would be visible from a dozen different hiding places, and so far as he could see it was undamaged. He tested the automatic mechanism, and for good measure ran the picture through one showing.

He had already tossed another can of food in the grass near the screen, and he was turning away when he thought, That's odd. The metal framework looks as if it's been polished.

He studied the phenomenon in a de-energizing mirror and saw that the metal had been covered with a clear, varnishlike substance. A dreadful sickness came over him as he recognized it. He decided in agony, If the cue is not to fire at all, I won't do it. I'll fire even if the blaster turns on me.

He scraped some of the "varnish" into a receptacle and began his retreat to the lifeboat. He was thinking violently, Where does he get all this stuff? That isn't part of the equipment of a survey craft.

The first suspicion was on him that what was happening was not just an accident. He was pondering the vast implications of that when off to one side he saw the Rull. For the first time, in his many days on the tableland, he saw the Rull.

What's the cue?

Memory of purpose came to the Rull shortly after he had eaten. It was a dim memory at first, but it grew stronger. It was not the only sensation of his returning energy. His visual centers interpreted more light. The starlit tableland grew brighter, not as bright as it could be for him, by a large percentage, but the direction was up instead of down. He felt unutterably fortunate that it was no worse.

He had been gliding along the edge of the precipice. Now he paused to peer down. Even with his partial light vision, the view was breath-taking. There was distance below and distance afar. From a spaceship, the effect of height was minimized. But gazing down that wall of gravel into those depths was a different experience. It emphasized how greatly he had suffered, how completely he had been caught by an accident. And it reminded him of what he had been doing before the hunger. He turned instantly away from the cliff and hurried to where the wreckage of his ship had gathered dust for days—bent and twisted wreckage, half buried in the hard ground of Laertes III. He glided over the dented plates inside to one in which he had the day before sensed a quiver of antigravity oscillation—tiny, potent, tremendous minutiae of oscillation, capable of being influenced.

The Rull worked with intensity and purposefulness. The plate was still firmly attached to the frame of the ship. And the first job, the extremely difficult job, was to tear it completely free. The hours passed.

With a tearing sound, the hard plate yielded to the slight rearrangement of its nucleonic structure. The shift was infinitesimal, partly because the directing nervous energy of his body was not at norm and partly because it was calculated to be small. There was such a thing as releasing energy enough to blow up a mountain.

Not, he discovered finally, that there was any danger in this plate. He found that out the moment he crawled onto it. The sensation of power that pulsed from it was so slight that, briefly, he doubted that it would lift from the ground. But it did. The test run lasted seven feet and gave him his measurement of the limited force he had available. Enough for an attack only.

There were no doubts in his mind. The experiment was over. His only purpose must be to kill the man, and the question was, how could he insure that the man did not kill him while he was doing it? The varnish!

He applied it painstakingly, dried it with a drier, and then, picking up the plate again, he carried it on his back to the hiding place he wanted. When he had buried it and himself under the dead leaves of a clump of brush, he grew calmer. He recognized that the veneer of his civilization was off. It shocked him, but he did not regret it. In giving him the food, the two-legged being was obviously doing something to him. Something dangerous. The only answer to the entire problem of the experiment of the tableland was to deal death without delay. He lay tense, ferocious, beyond the power of any vagrant thoughts, waiting for the man to come.

What happened then was as desperate a venture as Jamieson had seen in Service. Normally, he would have handled it expertly. But he was watching intently—for the paralysis to strike him. The paralysis that was of the varnish. And so, it was the unexpected normal act that confused him. The Rull flew out of a clump of trees mounted on the antigravity plate. The surprise of that was so great that it almost succeeded. The plates had been drained of all such energies, according to his tests, the first morning. Yet here was one alive again and light again with the special antigravity lightness which Rull scientists had brought to the peak of perfection.

The action of movement through space toward him was, of course, based on the motion of the planet as it turned on its axis. The speed of the attack, starting as it did from zero, did not come near the eight-hundred-mile-an-hour velocity of the spinning planet, but it was swift enough. The apparition of metal and reticulated Rull body charged at him through the air. And even as he drew his weapon and fired at it, he had a choice to make, a restraint to exercise: *Do not kill!*

That was hard, oh, hard. The necessity imposed a limitation so stern that during the second it took him to adjust, the Rull came to within ten feet of him. What saved him was the pressure of the air on the metal plate. The air tilted it like the wing of a plane becoming air-borne. He fired his irresistible weapon at the bottom of the metal plate, seared it, and deflected it to a crash landing in a clump of bushes twenty feet to his right. Jamieson was deliberately slow in following up his success. When he reached the bushes, the Rull was fifty feet beyond them and disappearing into a clump of trees. He did not pursue it or fire a second time. Instead, he gingerly pulled the Rull antigravity plate out of the brush and examined it.

The question was, how had the Rull degravitized it without the elaborate machinery necessary? And if it were capable of creating such a "parachute" for itself why hadn't it floated down to the forest far below, where food would be available and where it would be safe from its human enemy? One question was answered the moment he lifted the antigravity plate. It was about normal weight, its energy apparently exhausted after traveling less than a hundred feet. It had obviously never been capable of making the mile and a half trip to the forest and plain below.

Jamieson took no chances. He dropped the plate over the nearest precipice and watched it fall into distance. He was back in the lifeboat when he remembered the "varnish." There had been no cue; not yet. He tested the scraping he had brought with him. Chemically, it turned out to be simple resin, used to make varnishes. Atomically, it was stabilized. Electronically, it transformed light into energy on the vibration level of human thought. It was alive all right. But what was the recording? He made a graph of every material and energy level, for comparison purposes. As soon as he had established that it had been altered on the electronic level—which had been obvious but which, still, had to be proved—he recorded the images on a visiwire. The result was a hodgepodge of dreamlike fantasies.

Symbols. He took down his book, *Symbol Interpretations of the Unconscious*, and found the cross-reference:

"Inhibitions Mental." On the referred page and line, he read, "Do not kill!"

"Well, I'll be . . ." Jamieson said aloud into the silence of the lifeboat interior. "That's what happened."

He was relieved, and then not so relieved. It had been his personal intention not to kill at this stage. But the Rull hadn't known that. By working such a subtle inhibition, it had dominated the attack even in defeat. That was the trouble. So far he had gotten out of situations but had created no successful ones in retaliation. He had a hope, but that wasn't enough.

He must take no more risks. Even his final experiment must wait until the day the *Orion* was due to arrive. Human beings were just a little too weak in certain directions. Their very life cells had impulses which could be stirred by the cunning and the remorseless. He did not doubt that, in the final issue, the Rull would try to stir him toward self-destruction.

XXV

ON THE NINTH NIGHT, the day before the *Orion* was due, Jamieson refrained from putting out a can of food. The following morning he spent half an hour at the radio trying to contact the battleship. He made a point of broadcasting a detailed account of what had happened so far, and he described what his plans were, including his intention of testing the Rull to see if it had suffered any injury from its period of hunger.

Subspace was totally silent. Not a pulse of vibration

answered his call. He finally abandoned the attempt to establish contact and went outside and swiftly set up the instruments he would need for his experiment. The tableland had the air of a deserted wilderness. He tested his equipment, then looked at his watch. It was eleven minutes to noon. Suddenly jittery, he decided not to wait the extra minutes. He walked over, hesitated, and then pressed a button. From a source near the screen, a rhythm on a very high energy level was being broadcast. It was a variation of the rhythm pattern to which the Rull had been subjected for four nights. Slowly Jamieson retreated toward the lifeboat. He wanted to try again to contact the *Orion*. Looking back, he saw the Rull glide into the clearing and head straight for the source of the vibration. As Jamieson paused involuntarily, fascinated, the main alarm system of the lifeboat went off with a roar. The sound echoed with an alien eeriness on the wings of the icy wind that was blowing, and it acted like a cue. His wrist radio snapped on, synchronizing automatically with the powerful radio in the lifeboat.

A voice said urgently, "Trevor Jamieson, this is the *Orion*. We heard your earlier calls but refrained from answering. An entire Rull fleet is cruising in the vicinity of the Laertes sun. In approximately five minutes, an attempt will be made to pick you up. Meanwhile, *drop everything*."

Jamieson dropped. It was a physical movement, not a mental one. Out of the corner of one eye, even as he heard his own radio, he saw a movement in the sky: two dark blobs that resolved into vast shapes. There was a roar as the Rull super-battleships flashed by overhead. A cyclone followed their passage that nearly tore him from the ground, where he clung desperately to the roots of intertwining brush. At top speed, obviously traveling under gravitonic power, the enemy warships made a sweeping turn and came back toward the tableland. Jamieson expected death momentarily, but the fire flashed past; then the thunder of the released energies rolled toward him, a colossal sound, almost yet not quite submerging his awareness of what had happened. His lifeboat! They had fired at his lifeboat.

He groaned as he pictured it destroyed in one burst of intolerable flame. And then there was no time for thought of anguish.

A third warship came into view, but, as Jamieson strained to make out its contours, it turned and fled.

His wrist radio clicked on. "Cannot help you now. Save yourself. Our four accompanying battleships and attendant squadrons will engage the Rull fleet, and try to draw them toward our larger battle group cruising near the star, Bianca, and then re—"

A flash of fire in the distant sky ended the message. It was a full minute before the cold air of Laertes III echoed to the remote burst of the broadside. The sound died slowly, reluctantly, as if little overtones of it were clinging to each molecule of air. The silence that settled finally was, strangely, not peaceful, but a fateful, quiescent stillness, alive with unmeasurable threat.

Shakily, Jamieson climbed to his feet. It was time to assess the immediate danger that had befallen him. The greater danger he dared not even think about. He headed first for his lifeboat. He didn't have to go all the way. The entire section of the cliff had been sheared away. Of the ship, there was no sign. He had expected it, but the shock of the reality was numbing. He crouched like an animal and stared up into the sky. Not a movement was there, not a sound came out of it, except the sound of the east wind. He was alone in a universe between heaven and earth, a human being poised at the edge of an abyss.

Into his mind, tensely waiting, pierced a sharp understanding. The Rull ships had flown once over the mountain to size up the situation on the tableland and then had tried to destroy him. Equally disturbing and puzzling was the realization that battleships of the latest design were taking risks to defend his opponent on this isolated mountain.

He'd have to hurry. At any moment they might risk one of their destroyers in a rescue landing. As he ran, he felt himself one with the wind. He knew that feeling, that sense of returning primitiveness during moments of excitement. It was like that in battles, and the important thing was to yield one's whole body and soul to it. There was no such thing as fighting efficiently with half your mind or half your body. All was demanded.

He expected falls, and he had them. Each time he got up, almost unaware of the pain, and ran on again. He arrived bleeding, almost oblivious to a dozen cuts. And the sky remained silent.

From the shelter of a line of brush, he peered at the Rull. The captive Rull, *his* Rull to do with as he pleased. To watch, to force, to educate—the fastest education in the history of the world. There wasn't any time for a leisurely exchange of information. From where he lay, he manipulated the controls of the screen.

The Rull had been moving back and forth in front of the screen. Now it speeded up, then slowed, then speeded up again, according to his will.

Nearly a thousand years before, in the twentieth century, the classic and timeless investigation had been made of which this was one end result. A man called Pavlov fed a laboratory dog at regular intervals, to the accompaniment of the ringing of a bell. Soon the dog's digestive system responded as readily to the ringing of the bell without the food as to the food and the bell together. Pavlov himself did not, until late in his life, realize the most important reality behind this conditioning process. But what began on that remote day ended with a science that could brainwash animals, and aliens —and men—almost at will. Only the Rulls baffled the master experimenters in the later centuries when it was an exact science. Defeated by the will to death of all the Rull captives, the scientists foresaw the doom of Earth's galactic empire unless some beginning could be made in penetrating the minds of Rulls. It was his desperate bad luck that he had no time for penetrations. There was death here for those who lingered.

But even the bare minimum of what he had to do would take time. Back and forth, back and forth; the rhythm of obedience had to be established. The image of the Rull on the screen was as lifelike as the original. It was three-dimensional, and its movements were like those of an automaton. Basic nerve centers were affected. The Rull could no more help falling into step than it could resist the call of the food impulse. After it had followed that mindless pattern for fifteen minutes, changing pace at his direction, Jamieson started the Rull and its image climbing trees. Up, then down again, half a dozen times. At that point, Jamieson introduced an image of himself.

Tensely, with one eye on the sky and one on the scene before him, he watched the reactions of the Rull. When, after a few minutes, he substituted himself for his image, he was satisfied that this Rull had temporarily lost its normal hate and suicide conditioning when it saw a human being.

Now that he had reached the stage of final control, he hesitated. It was time to make his tests. Could he afford the time? He realized that he had to. This opportunity might not occur again in a hundred years.

When he finished the tests twenty-five minutes later, he was pale with excitement. He thought, This is it.

We've got it. He spent ten precious minutes broadcasting his discovery by means of his wrist radio—hoping that the transmitter on his lifeboat had survived its fall down the mountain—and was rebroadcasting the message out through subspace. There was not a single answer to his call, however, during the entire ten minutes.

Aware that he had done what he could, Jamieson headed for the cliff's edge he had selected as a starting point. He looked down and shuddered, then remembered what the *Orion* had said: "An entire Rull fleet cruising . . ."

Hurry!

He lowered the Rull to the first ledge. A moment later he fastened the harness around his own body and stepped into space. Sedately, with easy strength, the Rull gripped the other end of the rope and lowered him down to the ledge beside it. They continued on down and down. It was hard work, although they used a very simple system. A long plastic line spanned the spaces for them. A metal climbing rod held position after position while the rope did its work.

On each ledge, Jamieson burned the rod at a downward slant into solid rock. The rope slid through an arrangement of pulleys in the metal as the Rull and he, in turn, lowered to ledges farther down. The moment they were both safely in the clear of one ledge, Jamieson would explode the rod out of the rock, and it would drop down ready for use again. The day sank toward darkness like a restless man into sleep. Jamieson's whole being filled with the melancholy of the fatigue that dragged at his muscles.

He could see that the Rull was growing more aware of him. It still cooperated, but it watched him with intent eyes each time it swung him down. The conditioned state was ending. The Rull was emerging from its trance. The process should be complete before night.

There was a time, then, when Jamieson despaired of getting down before the shadows fell. He had chosen the western, sunny side for that fantastic descent down a sheer, brown and black cliff like no other in the known worlds of space. He watched the Rull with quick, nervous glances during the moments when they were together on a ledge.

At 4:00 P.M. Jamieson had to pause again for a rest. He walked to the side of the ledge away from the Rull and sank down on a rock. The sky was silent and windless now, a curtain drawn across the black space above, concealing what must already be the greatest Rull-human battle in ten years. It was a tribute to the five Earth battleships that no Rull ship had yet attempted to rescue the Rull on the tableland. Possibly, of course, they didn't want to give away the presence of one of their own kind.

Jamieson gave up the futile speculation. Wearily, he compared the height of the cliff above with the depth that remained below. He estimated they had come two thirds of the distance. He saw that the Rull had turned to face the valley. Jamieson turned and gazed with it. The scene, even from this reduced elevation, was still spectacular. The forest began a quarter of a mile from the bottom of the cliff, and it almost literally had no end. It rolled up over the hills and down into the shallow valleys. It faltered at the edge of a broad river, then billowed out again, and climbed the slopes of mountains that sprawled mistily in distance.

Time to get going again. At twenty-five minutes after six, they reached a ledge a hundred and fifty feet above the uneven plain. The distance strained the capacity of the rope, but the initial operation of lowering the Rull to freedom and safety was achieved without incident. Jamieson gazed down curiously at the creature. What would it do now that it was in the clear?

It merely waited. Jamieson stiffened. He was not taking any such chance as that. He waved imperatively at the Rull and took out his blaster. The Rull backed away, but only into the safety of a group of rocks. Blood-red, the sun was sinking behind the mountains. Darkness moved over the land. Jamieson ate his dinner, and as he was finishing, he saw a movement below. He watched as the Rull glided along close to the foot of the precipice, until it disappeared beyond an outjut of the cliff.

Jamieson waited briefly, then swung out on the rope. The descent strained his strength, but there was solid ground at the bottom. Three quarters of the way down, he cut his finger on a section of the rope that was unexpectedly rough. When he reached the ground, he noticed that his finger was turning an odd gray. In the dimness, it looked strange and unhealthy. As he stared at it, the color drained from his face. He thought in bitter anger, The Rull must have smeared it on the rope on the way down.

A pang went through his body and was followed instantly by a feeling of rigidity. With a gasp, he clutched at his blaster, intending to kill himself. His hand froze in mid-air. He toppled stiffly, unable to break his fall. There was the shock of contact with the hard ground, then unconsciousness.

The will to death is in all life. Every organic cell ecphorizes the inherited engrams of its inorganic origin. The pulse of life is a squamous film superimposed on an underlying matter so intricate in its delicate balancing of different energies that life itself is but a brief, vain straining against that balance. For an instant of eternity a pattern is attempted. It takes many forms, but these are apparent. The real shape is always a time and not a space shape. And that shape is a curve. Up and then down. Up from darkness into the light, then down again into the blackness.

The male salmon sprays his mist of milt onto the eggs of the female. And instantly he is seized with a mortal melancholy. The male bee collapses from the embrace of the queen he has won, back into that inorganic mold from which he climbed for one single moment of ecstasy. In man, the fateful pattern is impressed time and again into numberless ephermeral cells, but only the pattern endures.

The sharp-minded Rull scientist, probing for chemical substances that would shock man's system into its primitive forms, had, long before, found the special secret of man's will to death.

The *yeli*, Meeesh, gliding back toward Jamieson, did not think of the process. He had been waiting for the opportunity. It had occurred. Briskly, he removed the man's blaster; then he searched for the key to the lifeboat. Then he carried Jamieson a quarter of a mile around the base of the cliff to where the man's ship had been catapulted by the blast from the Rull warships. Five minutes later the powerful radio inside was broadcasting on Rull wave lengths an imperative command to the Rull fleet.

Dimness. Inside and outside his skin. Jamieson felt himself at the bottom of a well, peering out of night into twilight. As he lay, a pressure of something swelled around him, lifted him higher and higher, and nearer to the mouth of the well. He struggled the last few feet, a distinct mental effort, and looked over the edge. Consciousness.

He was lying on a raised table inside a room which had several large mouselike openings at the floor level, openings that led to other chambers. Doors, he identified, odd-shaped, alien, unhuman. Jamieson cringed with the stunning shock of recognition. He was inside a Rull warship.

He could not decide if the ship were in motion, but he guessed that it was. The Rull would not linger in the vicinity of a planet.

He was able to turn his head, and he saw that nothing material held him. Of such things he knew as much as any Rull, so in an instant he had located the source of gravitonic beams that interlaced across him.

The discovery was of abstract value, he realized bitterly. He began to nerve himself, then, for the kind of death that he could expect. Torture by experiment.

Nerving himself was a simple procedure. It had been discovered that if a man could contemplate every possible type of torture, and what he would do while it was occurring, and became angry rather than afraid, he could maintain himself to the very edge of death with a minimum of pain.

Jamieson was hurriedly cataloguing the types of torture he might receive when a plaintive voice said into his ear, "Let's go home, huh?"

It took a moment to recover; it took seconds to consider that the Ploian was probably invulnerable to energy blasts such as had been dealt his lifeboat by the Rull warship. And at least a minute went by before Jamieson said in a low voice, "I want you to do something for me."

"Of course."

"Go into that box over there and let the energy flow through you."

"Oh, goody. I've been wanting to go in there."

An instant later the electric source of the gravitonic beams was obviously rechanneled. For Jamieson was able to sit up. He moved hastily away from the box and called, "Come out."

It required several calls to attract the Ploian's attention. Then Jamieson asked, "Have you looked this ship over?"

"Yes," the Ploian replied.

"Is there a section through which all the electric energy is channeled?"

"Yes."

Jamieson drew a deep breath. "Go into it and let the energy flow through you. Then come back here."

"Oh, you're so good to me," the Ploian responded.

Jamieson took the precaution of hastily finding a nonmetallic object to stand on. He was barely in a safe position when a hundred thousand volts crackled from every metal plate.

"What now?" said the Ploian two minutes later.

"Look the ship over and see if any Rulls are alive."

Almost instantly, Jamieson was informed that about a hundred Rulls were still alive. From the reports of the Ploian, the survivors were already staying away from contact with metal surfaces. Jamieson accepted the information thoughtfully. Then he described the radio equipment to the Ploian, and finished, "Whenever anyone attempts to use this equipment, you go inside it and let the electricity flow through you—understand?"

The Ploian agreed to do this, and Jamieson added, "Report back to me periodically, but only at times when no one is trying to use the radio. And don't go into the main switchboard without my permission."

"Consider it done," the Ploian said.

Five minutes later the Ploian located Jamieson in the weapon room. "Somebody tried to use the radio just now; but he gave up finally, and went away."

"Fine," said Jamieson. "Keep watch—and listen—and join me as soon as I'm through here."

Jamieson proceeded on the positive assumption that he had one decisive advantage over the Rull survivors:

he knew when it was safe to touch metal. They would have to rig up elaborate devices before they could dare move.

In the weapon control room he worked with energy cutting tools, hurriedly but effectively. His purpose: to make certain that the gigantic blasters could not be fired until the weapon control wiring was totally repaired.

That job done, he headed for the nearest lifeboat. The Ploian joined him as he was edging his way through an opening.

"There're some Rulls that way," the Ploian warned. "Better go this way."

They finally entered a Rull lifeboat without mishap. A few minutes later Jamieson launched the small craft, but five days went by before they were picked up.

The high Aaish of Yeell was not on the ship to which Jamieson had been taken as a captive. And so he was not among the dead, and, indeed, did not learn of the escape of the prisoner for some time. When the information was finally brought to him, his staff took it for granted that he would punish the Rull survivors of the wrecked battleship.

Instead, he said thoughtfully, "So that was the enemy? A very powerful being."

He silently considered the week of anguish he had endured. He had recovered almost all of his perceptive powers—so he was able to have a very unusual thought for an individual of his high estate.

He said, using the light-wave communicator, "I believe that this is the first time that a Prime Leader has visited the battlefront. Is this not correct?"

It was correct. A Super-General had come from rear headquarters to the "front lines." Top brass had come out of the sheltered and protected home planet and risked a skin so precious that all of Ria shuddered anxiously when the news was released.

The greatest Rull continued his speculations: "It would seem to me that we have not received the most accurate intelligence about human beings. There appears to have been an attempt to underestimate their abilities, and while I commend the zeal and courage of such attempts, my reaction is that this war is not likely to be successful in any decisive way. It is therefore my conclusion that the Central Council re-examine the motives for the continuation of the battle effort. I do not foresee an immediate disengagement, but it might well be that the fighting could gradually dissipate, as we assume a defensive position in this area of space, and perhaps turn our attention to other galaxies."

Far away, across light-years of space, Jamieson was reporting to an august body, the Galactic Convention: "I feel that this was a Very Important Person among the Rulls; and, since I had him under complete hypnosis for some time, I think we should have a favorable reaction. I told him that the Rulls were underestimating human beings, and that the war would not be successful, and I suggested that they turn their attention to other galaxies."

Years were to pass before men would finally be certain that the Rull-human war was over. At the moment, the members of the convention were fascinated by the way in which a mind-reading baby ezwal had been used to contact an invisible Ploian; and of how this new ally had been the means of a human being escaping from a Rull battleship with such vital information as Jamieson had brought with him.

It was justification for all the hard years and patient effort that men had devoted to a policy of friendship with alien races. By an overwhelming majority the convention created for Jamieson a special position which would be called: Administrator of Races.

He would return to Carson's Planet as the ultimate alien authority, not only for ezwals, but as it turned out, the wording of his appointment was later interpreted to mean that he was man's negotiator with the Rull.

While these matters developed, the galactic-wide Rull-human war ended.